"I've come to say goodbye."

Charlotte had known it, but Curtis's words stunned her just the same. "Are you going to tell me why?"

"Because I can't handle it. Because it isn't fair to you. This. Us. It's pointless. We're on a road to nowhere." He looked away. "I can't marry you, Charlotte."

"I don't remember asking you to," Charlotte said. "But we're right together, you can't deny that."

"You or anyone else," he added, as though he hadn't heard her. "It wouldn't be fair."

She couldn't speak, couldn't utter a sound.

"I've never felt about any woman the way I feel about you, Charlotte. With you it would have to be all or nothing. And I'm living with something for which I can never forgive myself, from which I'll never be free."

CLAUDIA JAMESON lives in Berkshire, England, with her husband and family. She is an extremely popular author in both the Harlequin Presents and Harlequin Romance series. And no wonder! Her lively dialogue and ingenious plots—with the occasional dash of suspense—make her a favorite with romance readers everywhere.

Books by Claudia Jameson

HARLEQUIN ROMANCE
2578—NEVER SAY NEVER
2594—YOURS...FAITHFULLY
2691—A TIME TO GROW

HARLEQUIN PRESENTS
777—THE FRENCHMAN'S KISS
817—THE SCORPIO MAN
867—ROSES, ALWAYS ROSES
891—THE MAN IN ROOM 12
922—ONE DREAM ONLY
945—ADAM'S LAW
969—TO SPEAK OF LOVE

Don't miss any of our special offers. Write to us at the following address for information on our newest releases.

Harlequin Reader Service
901 Fuhrmann Blvd., P.O. Box 1397, Buffalo, NY 14240
Canadian address: P.O. Box 603,
Fort Erie, Ont. L2A 5X3

Immune
to Love
Claudia Jameson

Harlequin Books

TORONTO • NEW YORK • LONDON
AMSTERDAM • PARIS • SYDNEY • HAMBURG
STOCKHOLM • ATHENS • TOKYO • MILAN

Original hardcover edition published in 1986
by Mills & Boon Limited

ISBN 0-373-02842-3

Harlequin Romance first edition June 1987

For Ann and Don. Never one
without the other. Always a
couple. With love, and thanks
for all the ice-creams.

Printed in U.S.A.

CHAPTER ONE

THERE had been times when she wished she'd never heard the name Fernando Licer. But who in the art world hadn't heard it? The man had been dead for twenty-five years but, as is so often the case with artists, his fame was posthumous. And it was growing. Anyone who owned a painting, a drawing or even the most meagre of sketches by him would hang on to it if they had any sense at all.

Curtis Maxwell had a lot of sense.

Charlotte Graham stuck her elbows on her desk, examining very carefully, minutely, the proofs of the catalogue for the forthcoming exhibition of Licer's work. As she turned the last page she was smiling broadly, her unruly russet-red hair tumbling around her face as she shook her head from side to side. 'I don't believe it. I just don't believe it!' The pronouncement, and more particularly her tone of voice, brought her secretary's head up with a snap.

'What?' Linda Reed was taken aback. It wasn't like Charlie to speak with such emotion, or so she thought. To Linda her boss was the epitome of efficiency—capable, cool, calm and collected.

'These!' Charlie waved the sheaf of papers in the air. 'These proofs are the nearest to perfection I've ever seen. I mean, the printers have got it *right!*'

'Wonders will never, and all that,' Linda giggled, then returned her attention immediately to the letter she was typing.

Charlie watched her for a moment, looking at the dark head bowed in concentration as she transcribed shorthand to written English, her fingers flying across the keys of her typewriter. Linda was a gem. It was,

Charlotte thought, unfair, really. Linda would be perfectly capable of doing Charlie's job as well as Charlie herself, but she might not. This was because Charlie had a degree and Linda hadn't. That was the way of the world. Charlie was actually Charlotte Amanda Graham, B.A., Bachelor of Arts. Three years in a polytechnic in Newcastle had earned her those letters after her name.

She was employed as co-ordinator and personal assistant to Mr Edward Grant, director and top dog in the College Gallery. The College Gallery was part of—belonged to—the art school to which it was attached. It was non-profit-making and the forthcoming exhibition would be their biggest and best yet. In fact it was pretty ambitious for a gallery of its size.

Though there had been days when Charlie had wished she'd never heard the name Fernando Licer, today wasn't one of them. There had been so much to do, so much preparation involved. As a co-ordinator, she had spent weeks—several of them—co-ordinating! She looked again, very carefully, at the proofs, unable to believe that at long last things were going smoothly.

'Fernando Licer.' She spoke the name inaudibly as she continued her scrutiny, checking and rechecking. The artist had died at the age of fifty, twenty-five years earlier. He had been half English, half Spanish. His formative years had been spent in Spain, in poverty, in a northern village with an unpronounceable name. At thirteen he had run away from home and vanished for several years, travelling and doing heaven knew what to earn a crust. Details of those years of the artist's life were vague. At nineteen he had reappeared, this time in England where he was to remain, and indeed had spent some time at the art school, at this very establishment. Which was why next month's exhibition would be particularly interesting and successful.

In this respect, the gallery owed many thanks to

- Curtis Maxwell, among others. He had lent seven Licer paintings to them for the exhibition, all of which were from his private collection. And all seven of them, according to Charlie's boss, had a special meaning for their owner. So his lending them was a kind gesture indeed because there were always risks involved in transportation and handling. It was open to question whether or not Curtis Maxwell would have loaned his valuable paintings had he not been a personal friend of Mr Grant. Charlie would never know the answer to that. She knew little about the man, had never met him and had spoken to him only once, and very briefly, on the telephone one day when her boss was off the premises. It was Mr Grant, not she, who had dealt with Mr Maxwell. Apart from that one short conversation, the closest she had got to him was when she'd passed on messages to his secretary, or taken messages from her.

Of course she had been familiar with Maxwell's name for a long time, since before she started this job just over a year ago. He owned several art galleries in London, his head office being at his Mayfair branch. Charlotte knew them all, had browsed in all of them over the two years she'd lived in London—not that she could afford the sort of art the Maxwell galleries dealt in. The paintings she would like to own would never, could never, belong to the likes of her. Her appreciation of art was profound, her personal tastes expensive, but her salary was small! She had earned more money as a temp than she was earning here at the gallery. Still, she loved her job.

There was one painting of Licer's, belonging to Curtis Maxwell, which Charlie had fallen in love with on sight. It was called *The Lady in White* and it was a portrait of a beautiful, fair-haired woman of early middle age. Who the woman was, was anybody's guess. If Mr Grant knew, he hadn't said so when Charlotte admired the painting. It had been delivered to the gallery along with the other six as soon as she had finalised the details of their insurance, in order that they could be photographed for the catalogue. She had gasped in admiration when she first saw it.

'It's beautiful! *She's* beautiful! I wonder who she is?' She had looked from the portrait to her boss. Mr Grant had said nothing, had appeared not to have heard Charlie's remarks, her question.

Turning her attention back to the painting, she and Edward Grant had gazed at it for minutes. Not wishing to disturb his reverie, Charlie kept the rest of her thoughts and questions to herself. This painting! It was so very lovely. It was vaguely impressionist in as much as the edges of reality were removed. There was no doubt that the subject was a beautiful woman, but—there was something added ... no, not added but extra. A quality which made Charlie feel sure, absolutely sure, that Fernando Licer had been in love with his model.

When at length her boss spoke, it was with a dreamy inflection. 'You should see the rest of Curtis's private collection, Charlotte.'

She'd love to! She didn't say this, she thought it, smiling inwardly at the unmistakable envy in her boss's voice. Another art lover, Mr Grant was a man of few words ... *was* a man of few words. That is to say, he had been a man of few words—until a few weeks ago ...

'Charlie? What's up? Have you spotted some dire mistake? You're not just frowning, you're ageing yourself by the minute! Why so serious?'

Charlie looked up to find her secretary watching her, a look of concern on her face. She laughed. 'No, no, there's nothing. At least, if there are any mistakes I haven't spotted, I'm not likely to spot them at this stage. I know these proofs off by heart now and I'm not "seeing" them any more, if you know what I mean.'

Linda nodded obligingly. 'So why the frown?'

'I was thinking about Mr Grant.'

There was another obliging nod before Linda's face split into a broad grin. 'He's having some kind of second childhood, if you ask me!'

At the unintended joke, or near joke, they both laughed. Charlie's eyes, almost brown, almost hazel, and flecked with gold when the light was on them, widened and sparkled. They were gorgeous, fascinating eyes, not that she ever thought about it. But that's what people told her. Her features and her colouring were very striking. With hair of a most unusual hue, russet-red and naturally streaked with some strands of amber, darkest gold and copper, her skin by contrast seemed even whiter than it was. Smooth and soft to the touch, it was also freckled—and oh, how she hated those freckles! In her own opinion her looks were far from special, thanks to the freckles, which were scattered everywhere and not just on her face. But, again, people had been telling her all her life what a very attractive girl she was. At twenty-three she could now amend that to *woman*, perhaps. But attractive? Well, she was striking because she was a little different, that was all. There were lots of things she would alter if she could. She would rather be without the wretched freckles, she would rather be five feet four than five feet eight, and have fuller, *bigger* breasts! She would rather be ten or twelve pounds heavier, have curves instead of angles. But there was nothing to be done about this—any of it. She was as she was and she didn't lack confidence simply because she wasn't her own ideal woman. There were some advantages to the way she was made. Clothes always looked good on her, for one thing.

She sobered as Linda turned back to her typing, all laughter fading from both of them. It was time to go and see Mr Grant. Linda's unintended joke was ... well, in brief Mr Grant had undergone some sort of personality change a few weeks earlier. He had come in one morning, stood in the outer office which Charlotte and Linda shared, and announced in a voice and manner not at all normal for him, 'Well, girls, have I got news for you! I'm going to be a father! How does *that* grab you?' And with that, he'd thumped himself on the chest (no doubt because he couldn't reach to pat himself on the back), and stood grinning like the idiot he certainly was not. 'Well, Charlie? Linda? What do you have to say?'

Both Charlotte and Linda had been unable to say anything. They were thrilled for him, of course, each being fond of him in her own way. But this was not their Mr Grant. Fifty-one years old, sober and serious in the extreme, the director of the gallery was not given to the use of the vernacular of the young any more than he was known for his grinning—any more than he called Charlotte Charlie.

It was a first. All of it was a first! Including the baby. Hence his unprecedented display of excitement and gaiety. Poor Mr Grant. Lucky Mr Grant! Both girls had congratulated him heartily, sincerely, smiling with him as well as at him. That he had been married (and for the first time) only three years, they had both known. They had known he was married to a woman twenty years his junior; indeed they'd met Janice Grant two or three times. What they hadn't known was that the couple had intended to have, indeed had been trying desperately for, a family. How could they have known such personal details? Mr Grant was not the type to talk about his private life, just as he never pried into anyone else's. But on this auspicious morning, he had spoken for the first time of how he had wanted a child since the day he'd married Janice. It had been very touching, really, not to mention startling.

Since then, Edward Grant had not returned to his old self. Normally he was careful, pedantic in his job, an absolute stickler for detail, for making sure everything was done right, promptly and without fuss, for checking and checking again. Now he was—well, a little forgetful on occasion, to say the least! Lately it was Charlie who was chasing him up on certain matters, instead of vice versa. He also paused, now, to pass the time of day, to make small talk or to crack jokes. And most of the time they weren't funny ones, which was why Charlotte and Linda were still bemused. For herself, Charlie would be relieved when her boss became normal again. She didn't know what to expect of him at the moment. It was all very unsettling in a way; she felt a bit insecure.

'We've bought the pram. Got it on Saturday.' This was Edward Grant's greeting as Charlotte walked into his office. It was the first time she'd seen him this Monday morning; as usual he'd arrived at work before she had.

'Well! You don't let the grass grow, do you?' Charlie smiled, walked straight over to his desk and placed the proofs in front of him. Pointedly.

'It's navy blue—a de luxe model, of course—with a white canopy with a navy blue and white fringe.'

'It sounds ...' What could one say about a perambulator? '... very nice.'

'The cot won't be delivered until next month. I told you that, didn't I? That we'd ordered one? Thought so. We'll be ready in good time though, everything will be ready. Janice has picked out the wallpaper for the nursery and we'll get cracking on that next weekend. Or rather, I will. I've told her she's got to take it easy.'

He could be talking to himself, Charlie thought, but not unkindly. She was happy for him, very much so. But he was looking at the window now, not at her, as if fascinated by the raindrops trickling down it. She looked at the back of his greying, balding head and wondered about him. Married at forty-eight. Why so late? There was a story there somewhere; she would never know. Had he loved before Janice, loved and lost, perhaps? And what about this baby? Was he, beyond his excitement, also anxious at becoming a father at the age of fifty-one? Probably.

Quite suddenly, with his back still to her, he said, 'I never intended to marry, you know.'

'Mr Grant——' For some reason, Charlie was embarrassed suddenly. Curious though she was, this change in him was—was something difficult to get used to. 'The proofs came today. I've been over them with a fine-tooth comb and——'

'But I'm not immune. Nobody's immune.'

'Immune?' She gave up. She lowered herself gracefully into a chair, folded her arms across her chest and waited.

Mr Grant swung round in his swivel chair, looking at her as though she'd said something stupid. 'To love. I fell in love. And that, my dear, was that.'

'I see.'

'Have you ever been in love?'

What a question! Another first. She shook her head.

'Then no, you don't see.' He spoke categorically, defying contradiction.

Charlie had no intention of contradicting him. Not only did she not want to, it would have been pointless. Gosh, his mood was stranger than ever today! She gestured towards the proofs. 'Will you go over the proofs? I know we promised Mr Maxwell a copy as soon as we got them.'

The use of Curtis Maxwell's name wrought another change in her boss. He became, at least momentarily, what he was: the director of the gallery. 'Right, see to it. See he gets a copy straight away.'

Charlie got to her feet. 'If you'll let me know as soon as you've checked them——'

'Didn't you just tell me you'd been over them with a fine-tooth comb?'

So he had heard her! 'Yes, a dozen times. I promise you,' she added wryly, 'we can send them to Mr Maxwell with impunity.'

'Try using an envelope.'

'What? I——' Oh, Lord, another of his daft jokes! She forced a smile. 'I'll post them as soon as you've been over them.'

Surprising her yet again, Mr Grant pushed the proofs towards her. 'That's O.K. I trust you, you know that.'

Yes, she knew that. In the year that she had worked for him, she had never ever minded his checking up on her, so it was too much, now, for her to accept without protest his disinclination to go over the proofs himself. She refused outright; this exhibition was too important. And for another thing, Mr Grant had told her on more than one occasion that anything she did pertaining to Curtis Maxwell's paintings, anything at all, had to be *right*. There were seven of them and they were depicted in the proofs of the catalogue, with details about them. No, no way was she going to send a copy to him before her boss had looked them over!

'All right.' Edward nodded, took hold of the proofs and got down to it immediately. 'You're right, of course.'

Satisfied, she left him to get on with it.

Ten minutes later he came into her office. 'They're fine, Charlotte. In fact, they're the best I've seen. Printers must have had a brainstorm. I didn't spot anything you hadn't already spotted. You can get a copy off to Curtis straight away. But don't post them, send them in a taxi—no, on second thoughts, you take them. I've got a parcel for him in my office and it's fragile. I'd rather you handled it. In fact, now's as good a time as any.' And with that he went back into his office and fetched the parcel.

She could have walked to Maxwell's head office in Mayfair. Just. But it would have taken too long and

she had a lot to do. Besides, London was so crowded
with tourists, she didn't want to get jostled and drop
the parcel with its fragile contents.

Thanks to the rain, it was with difficulty that she
found a cab. She stood on the street, umbrella in one
hand, handbag containing the proofs in the crook of
her arm, parcel in the other hand, and wondered why
she hadn't thought to delegate this task to Linda.

Once inside the warmth and luxury of the Maxwell
Gallery, Charlie identified herself to an assistant and
was directed through the back of the shop, up two
flights of stairs to the offices. There was another floor
above, presumably a flat since there was a door at the
foot of the next flight of stairs. A door marked private.
Mr Maxwell's private flat? His home in the city?
Maybe he was a bachelor? She had no idea. No, that
wasn't likely. Not many men got to Mr Maxwell's age
without marrying.

That was how Charlie's mind was working—or
rather idling—as she walked into the office on the
second floor. She knocked and opened the first door
she came to. There were three of them, all unmarked.

There was a surprise in store for her. 'Margaret!
Maggie! What on earth are you doing here?'

She was answered with a broad smile as the other
girl's eyebrows shot up. 'We-ll, I might ask you the
same thing!' Maggie's Australian twang was laced with
laughter and surprise. 'Who are you, Charlie? I
mean—oh, you know what I mean! Where've you
come from?'

It was minutes before they sorted themselves out.
The two hadn't seen one another for over a year,
nearer to two in fact. They had worked for the same
employment agency, the one Charlotte had joined
after moving to London. She had spent a lot of time
looking for the right job, temping in the meantime,
and Margaret Banner and she had done a four-week
stint together in the offices of a commercial estate

agency in the City. And very boring it had been, for Charlie at least. Having no shorthand or typing skills, unlike Margaret, she had been obliged to take work as a filing clerk from time to time.

'The College Gallery.'

'Oh.' The words clearly didn't mean anything to Maggie. 'It's in Knightsbridge. It isn't a commercial concern like Maxwell's, it's part of the art school.'

'Ah, so you're working there these days? Permanent, I take it?'

'For just over a year, and I love it. It's the job I'd been looking for for months. And you? How come you're here?' Charlie gestured around the office, noting the communicating door to the next room. She lowered her voice, assuming the other office to be occupied. 'Who's in there, Curtis Maxwell? His secretary?'

'*I'm* Mr Maxwell's secretary.' There was another grin at Charlie's look of bewilderment. Margaret Banner's was not the voice she had spoken to from time to time. With her unmistakable Australian accent, there was no room for confusion.

'Since when?'

'Two weeks and . . .' Maggie looked at her watch. '. . . almost half a day.'

'But——'

'I'm temping, you idiot. Still temping. Mr Maxwell's secretary is ill. Poor thing's got shingles. She's been off for three weeks so far.'

'Shingles? Ooh, nasty! My father had that once, when I was little. It's painful.' She glanced again at the communicating door, a little worriedly this time.

'It's all right,' Maggie assured her. 'There's nobody in there. That's the big man's office, but he's never here Monday mornings. He'll be here after lunch if you want to see him——'

'No, not necessarily.' Charlie pulled the envelope from her bag and put the other girl in the picture, explaining about the loan of the paintings, since it was obvious Margaret knew nothing about it. 'And these are proofs of the catalogue,' she finished. 'He wanted to see a copy a soon as poss.'

Margaret nodded, unmoved, uninterested. There was a gleam in her eye which Charlie was at a loss to understand. 'What do you make of him?'

'Mr Maxwell? I've never met him, actually. I've spoken to him once, briefly, and that's it. I must say he sounded very curt.'

There was a shriek of laughter. 'That's what I've privately tagged him, Curtis the Curt! Do you know, the week before I came here, he had four temps in five days. He's a devil to work for!'

Charlie blinked in amazement. 'So why do you stay? You're a temp, you can drop out if——'

'As it happens, the job's interesting. Varied, never a dull moment. He's a hard taskmaster, but I don't mind, really. He's a bit like the Aussies, he works hard and he plays hard.'

Unconsciously Charlotte's head cocked to one side. She sat on the edge of Margaret's massive, expensive desk, her interest caught. That gleam was still in the other girl's eye. It was infectious. Charlie was grinning now. 'How can you know so much when you've only been here two weeks? I happen to know Mr Maxwell moves around a lot, this might be head office, but he isn't always here.'

'True. But I have to know his movements, haven't I? He keeps me informed all the time. Right now, for example, I happen to know he's in the Cotswolds with his little lady . . .' She broke off, deliberately adding to the intrigue by looking at her watch again. 'I'll amend that. He'll actually be driving back to London right now.'

'His little lady?'

Even knowing they were in no danger of being overheard, Margaret dropped her voice. 'He's got a

mistress tucked away! I've spoken to her myself.
Sexiest voice you ever heard! She's phoned here twice
since I've worked for him, goes by the name of Chris.
Just Chris. "Just tell him it's Chris," she says.
Anyhow, he leaves here at lunchtime every Friday and
comes back Monday lunch. He gave me the phone
number in the Cotswolds, said I could reach him there
if there were ever an emergency of any kind.'

This was wrong, this sort of gossip. Charlie knew it
but she couldn't help being intrigued. 'So he is a
bachelor——'

'Confirmed, from what I can gather.'

Charlie smiled, thinking of the words her boss had
used only a short time ago. Mr Maxwell might have
made it into his fifties without being snared, but,
'Nobody's immune.'

'Eh?'

There was laughter as Charlie shook her curly
head. 'Sorry—I was on a different train of thought.' It
was her turn to look at her watch. 'I'd better get back
to work.'

'Well, look, it's almost half-twelve. You have a
lunch hour, why not take it now and we can pop out
for a bite together? Catch up on what we've been
doing since——'

'Sorry.' She wasn't particularly. Though she had
worked with Margaret for a month, and had liked her,
they weren't friends as such, had never kept in touch,
because basically they had nothing in common.
Charlotte's social life was different from Margaret's,
considerably different. Margaret went out all the time,
partying, drinking, mixing with people, whereas
Charlie's private life was a quiet one except for her
involvement in amateur dramatics. 'I have a date for
lunch.'

It was Maggie who was intrigued now. 'Someone
special?'

'No, no. Geoffrey Hemmings, my neighbour.'

'So you're still seeing him? I remember the name——'

'Don't make anything of it,' came the swift reply. 'There's nothing to it. We belong to the local amateur dramatic society, if you remember.'

'I remember.' Maggie was unimpressed. 'So you're still involved with that scene.'

'I enjoy it.' Charlotte wasn't defensive, just making a statement of fact. 'Whatever turns you on, as they say.'

'It takes all kinds, as they also say.' There was a good-natured smile from the other girl. 'Ah, well, some other time, perhaps. It's been nice seeing . . .'

As their conversation came to a close, neither girl was aware they were being watched, that they had been watched for a full minute. Both of them had glanced from time to time at the door connecting Maggie's office to that of the boss, but neither of them had turned to look at the door to the corridor. And it was there that Curtis Maxwell stood, silently, leaning against the door jamb, his hands shoved deep into the pockets of his trousers, his expression impassive.

'It was nice seeing you, too.' Only as Charlotte slid her bottom from the desk was Margaret able to see the outer door. She cleared her throat noisily, an unnatural sound which made Charlotte look quickly at her. Registering at once the sudden tension in Maggie's face, Charlotte turned warily, nervously, following her eyes to the doorway.

It was with a swift, thankfully silent, intake of breath that Charlotte straightened to her full height, her hands automatically smoothing the skirt of the emerald-green suit she was wearing. Not for an instant did it occur to her that the man in the doorway was Curtis Maxwell. Crazily, such an idea didn't enter her head, despite the circumstances. She thought he was a customer or someone else who wanted to see the gallery owner. That was her automatic assumption. In the seconds before anything was said, however, she had time to register fully the shocking handsomeness of the man who had been eavesdropping. Blond, blue-eyed, he shifted his gaze coldly from Maggie to Charlie. He didn't move a muscle, he just looked, his massive frame almost filling the doorway; he had to be six feet three, at least.

Margaret was doing it again, clearing her throat nervously. 'Ah, Mr Maxwell. I understand you haven't met Miss Graham—Charlie Graham from the College Gallery.'

Charlie's mouth fell open in the most ungainly, undignified manner. Her eyes swivelled to those of the other girl, thinking she was joking. But Margaret wasn't joking. Nor was she looking at Charlie. She was watching the man anxiously, pushing her way through the rest of the introduction. 'Charlie, this is Curtis Maxwell . . .'

Charlie was as motionless now as the man in the doorway. Tunnel vision. She had been thinking in tramlines. How—*why* had she assumed Curtis Maxwell to be the same age as Edward Grant? He was years younger! Why had she assumed for all this time that because the two men were friends they were contemporaries? It didn't follow, of course it didn't follow!

She moved towards him, her hand outstretched, regaining her composure with difficulty. 'Mr Maxwell, how do you——'

'*Charlie?*' He cut her off rudely, ignoring her hand, his eyes riveted on hers. And still his scrutiny was cold, his eyes like blue chips of ice. 'What kind of name is that?'

CHAPTER TWO

'CHARLOTTE.' Her hand dropped to her side. 'I—it's Charlotte.'

'Well, Charlotte, what are you doing here?' Very clearly his question went on, 'Apart from gossiping with my secretary?' though the latter part was unspoken.

She had her back to Margaret now, but if the other girl felt anything like she did, she was uncomfortable. Charlie felt as though she'd been caught doing something naughty. She resented it, but doing so didn't help her one bit. 'I'm—I've brought a parcel for you from Mr Grant. And the copy of the proofs you wanted. The proofs of the catalogue.'

'I gathered you meant the proofs of the catalogue, Charlotte,' he said smoothly. 'And so?'

'And so I'll—be on my way now.' At least, she would if he would get out of her path! He was still blocking the doorway with his impressive and immaculately clad bulk. 'If you'll excuse me.' Deliberately she lowered her eyes, knowing she couldn't allow her feeling of animosity to show in them. She didn't like his attitude, didn't like it at all.

'I can take it they're in order, Charlotte, the proofs?'

'Of course!' Indignation rose to the fore. He couldn't possibly think she'd bring them if they weren't word perfect, could he? And they were, as far as his paintings were concerned, anyhow. All annotations, dates and details of his paintings were correct. She'd made absolutely sure of that.

'Splendid.' He spoke without inflection, standing aside finally to let her pass. 'Good day, Charlotte.'

She had unlocked herself from his gaze again.

Turning to wave briefly at Margaret, she hurried along the corridor and down the stairs, feeling hot and cross with herself. How much had he heard of her conversation with Margaret? For heaven's sake, he hadn't heard what had been said about him and his mistress, had he?

It was her own fault. She *had* been gossiping, or at least listening to it. The annoying thing was that she was as interested in the private life of Curtis Maxwell as she was in the man in the moon! What did she care whether he worked hard and played hard, whether he had a mistress, or two, or twenty? She didn't. She had been intrigued only because she'd taken it for granted that Curtis Maxwell was the same age, and the same type, as her boss.

Now that she'd met him, it surprised her not in the least that he was a womaniser. If that was a fair description. A man with his looks was ... but what was she worrying about? Why had she allowed herself to get so flustered, to be seen to be flustered? She should have coped with the shock instead of standing there like an open-mouthed idiot.

Idiot!

And, worse, she had very nearly been rude to him. How tempting it had been! It didn't matter that he had been rude to her, which he had ...

Charlotte walked briskly back to work. It was still raining but only slightly. She buttoned the jacket of her suit, cursing the English summer. It was early June, though who would guess it? The sky was grey and there was a chill wind blowing. She walked on, glancing at her watch again. She would make it back to the office in time to meet Geoffrey. Just. It was as quick to walk as to fight for a cab.

No, not rude, exactly. Sarcastic. He had used her name with every sentence he'd spoken to her. *Charlotte.* He'd said it slowly, as if to point out that neither she nor anyone else should refer to her as Charlie.

Back at the office, she was surprised to find that Geoffrey wasn't there. It was five past one and he was normally punctual. It was only when she spotted the note on her desk that she realised her plans had been changed for her. Linda's note was typed, perfectly and briefly. 'Gone to lunch,' it said. 'So's Mr Grant. Geoffrey phoned to say he can't make it, that he'll explain tonight.' There was a P.S. 'I've taken your white suit, will drop it off at the dry cleaners for you, save you going out in the rain again.'

Grunting, Charlie sat down. That was a kind gesture on Linda's part but she'd have to go out to get a sandwich. She wasn't the type who could go all day without eating something. In any case, she'd been so busy, she'd forgotten about her suit. Since she was never home before her local dry-cleaners closed, she took things to work and used the one in the next street if she was in a hurry for things and she needed her suit for the wedding in Kendal this coming weekend.

Still at odds with herself, still disturbed by her encounter with Curtis Maxwell, she got to her feet just as the phone rang.

'I thought you had a lunch date?'

The voice was at once familiar, it was just that she couldn't understand his ringing now. 'Mr Maxwell?'

'None other. Well, Charlotte?' There it was again, that stress on her name.

'I—my date was cancelled. I—Mr Grant's out, I'm afraid. He'll be back around two.'

There was no comment on that. 'On second thoughts, perhaps Charlie is more appropriate, after all.'

'I beg your pardon?' She was on her mettle. Something was coming, she could sense it. His voice had changed yet again. While a moment ago there had been sarcasm tinged with humour, now there was sarcasm tinged with anger.

'You heard. A right Charlie, I believe is the expression. Or is it a proper Charlie?'

The gesture was wasted because she had no audience, but she found herself holding the receiver away from her ear and glaring at it. Parrot-like, she said again, 'I beg your pardon?'

'What do they say in your part of the world?'

'My part of the world?'

'Well,' he drawled, 'that's better than a repetition of your last sentence. The North. Don't I hear a slight tinge of the North in your voice?'

That didn't please her, either. It was irrelevant that he was correct. Charlotte liked to think that her voice was without any trace of accent. As an amateur actress, it pleased her to think she could adopt or drop accents at will. Very politely, for she had to bear in mind who this man was and what he meant to her boss, she said, 'You have something on your mind, Mr Maxwell? A query?'

'A complaint.' There was no beating about the bush now, no attempt to conceal his annoyance. 'These proofs of yours——'

'What about them?' She couldn't believe it. 'Mr Maxwell, I'm aware there are some errors but as far as your paintings are concerned——'

'There's a major error.' He cut in on her as she'd cut in on him. *The Lady in White.* Have you got a copy of the proofs in front of you?'

Indeed she had, she was already turning to page forty-three and in a split second she had found it, her eyes scanning the notation, which was very short in this particular case: *The Lady in White.* Fernando Licer, undated. On loan from the Maxwell Galleries, London. 'There's nothing wrong with the notation, Mr Maxwell. I've just——'

'Everything's wrong,' he snapped. 'Don't tell me, I'm telling you! I very specifically instructed—I put it in writing, too—that as far as this painting's

concerned, there has to be no mention of the source of
the loan. I do *not* want to advertise my ownership of it.
Have you got that?'

Charlotte heard it but she didn't get it. A dozen
questions flitted through her mind. Mainly she wanted
to ask, why not? Of course she didn't dare. He had his
reasons, obviously. 'But——'

'But nothing, woman! Cut out the mention of
Maxwell Galleries and put what you should have put
in the first place—Private Collection. Nothing more.'

Seized with anger at his tone, it was all she could do
not to blurt at him that she knew nothing about his
'specific instruction'. *Who* had he told? *Where* was his
letter?

The answer was obvious. Charlotte's eyes moved to
the door of her boss's office. She would not, however,
be disloyal to Mr Grant by telling Curtis Maxwell she
had been given no such instruction herself, that she
had never seen his letter about *The Lady in White*.

Gritting her teeth, she apologised instead. 'I'm
terribly sorry, Mr Maxwell. Please accept my apologies
for this oversight, I'll see that it's rectified immediately.'

'Do that. And stick to your agreement in the future.'

'I'm—not sure what you mean.' Not sure? She
hadn't the first clue!

'I mean I don't want my name mentioned to the
press on the night of the preview, that's what I mean!
You really are a Charlie, aren't you?'

She closed her eyes, struggling for control. What a
nerve! Edward Grant, she said silently, this is your
fault, not mine. Cautiously, not wishing to add to his
conviction of her incompetence, she said, 'Of course I
know that, Mr Maxwell. It's—you mean only as far as
this particular painting's concerned, don't you?'

The answer to that was a growl. 'Oh, for God's
sake!' And with it, he hung up on her.

Stunned, Charlotte looked at the phone long after
the line had gone dead. He had actually hung up!

Infuriated, she slammed it back on to its cradle. She shot to her feet, wishing Linda were there so she could give vent to her emotions, so she could tell of the injustice of it all. What was so special about *The Lady in White*? Not that it mattered. More to the point, *why* hadn't Edward passed on the instructions about it? When the other six paintings were annotated as being on loan from the Maxwell Galleries, why should the ownership of this one remain anonymous? Again, that didn't matter, was none of her business. What mattered was that she *hadn't been told*.

She never did get any lunch. She sat at her desk and fretted, following Mr Grant through to his office as soon as he came back. By then she had worked herself into a lather and was more upset than the situation called for. 'Mr Grant . . .' Launching immediately into her story, Charlotte was horrified to realise that tears were stinging the back of her eyes.

'I'm sorry, Charlotte.' Edward's apology was swift, without defence. 'It's my fault, all of it.'

Somehow, that didn't help much. It was *she* who had had to withstand the scorn of Curtis Maxwell. 'He was most unpleasant,' she protested. 'Very rude indeed!' she went on, reporting his remarks about the press on preview night. 'I mean, if I'd realised, if I'd been told, fair enough! But how was I to know he wanted the ownership of that painting kept secret? And why should he, for heaven's sake?'

'I don't know. Maybe because it's his mother. I dare say that has something to do with it.'

'His mother?' Charlotte stared at him. Was this another of her boss's silly jokes? 'His *mother? The Lady in White?*'

'Yes. Oh, I don't know!' Edward threw up his hands, sincerely at a loss. 'He's never spoken to me about it except to tell me it's his mother. I don't know him all that well, Charlotte, but I can tell you that in some ways he's a strange man.'

'I thought you and he were friends?'

'Well, yes, but there are friends and friends. I first met him seven years ago, when I took over here. My relationship with him is more business than social. He's been giving money annually to the school for years. Didn't you know that?'

'No, I didn't!' The finances of the art school had nothing to do with her. 'Oh, crumbs!'

'What is it? You weren't rude to him, were you? I shouldn't like to think——'

'No, no. It's just—just that I wish I'd known more about our benefactor, that's all.'

'I'm sorry,' Edward said again. 'Now sit yourself down and I'll ring him, explain it was my neglect——'

'No!' Pulling herself together, she relented totally. She shouldn't be all that surprised over this—hadn't Edward been in a world of his own these past few weeks? 'It doesn't matter. I know now, that's all that matters. Frankly, I don't care what Curtis Maxwell thinks of me.'

'Well, I do!' Her boss looked at her sharply. 'I care because you represent the gallery. We have an image to maintain. I don't want anything in any way to jeopardise ...' He left the rest of the sentence unspoken.

Charlotte did not. 'Mr Maxwell's philanthropy.'

'If that's cynicism I hear in your voice, it's unfair. He is a philanthropist. It's something he never talks about, but you can take my word on it. There are two loves in Curtis's life. One of them is art.'

And the other? Women, no doubt!

She headed for the door, turning to add one more comment because she simply couldn't resist doing so. 'I wouldn't mind so much, Mr Grant, if you yourself hadn't checked those proofs. But you did!'

'I know, I know!' Her boss held up his hands, his consistent lack of argument taking the wind out of her sails completely. She went back to her office to find

Linda sitting there, for once making no attempt at work.

'What was that all about? Raised voices, yet! I've never seen you as ruffled as you are today, Charlie! What's wrong?'

'Curtis Maxwell,' she began, seeing no reason why she shouldn't tell her secretary the tale. 'No, it's——' She nodded in the direction of the boss's door. 'It's Mr Grant, really.'

Linda was smiling benignly. 'He's beautiful, isn't he?'

It took two seconds for Charlie to pick up on Linda's mind. She wasn't talking about Edward, that was for sure! 'Beautiful?' Wasn't that too strong a word? Handsome, certainly. Striking, definitely, but beautiful? Even if he were, she was too biased to be able to see it. She had disliked the man from the moment he'd first spoken to her. 'I didn't know you'd met him.'

'Several times, not that he grants us an audience often, or even regularly.'

Charlotte nodded. Of course Linda must have met him. She'd worked at the gallery far longer than Charlie had.

By the end of the day, she was for once eager to get out of the office, for once wishing she didn't have to go to rehearsal that night. But she did have to rehearse. The Park Lane Players' latest effort was to be staged in the not too distant future and rehearsals had been stepped up from three to four nights a week.

They were doing *Count Your Regrets at Midnight*, and Charlotte had the lead, the role of a somewhat ageing prostitute who hates what she's doing but who knows no other way of earning a living. Geoffrey was the male lead, between them they had fourteen rather long speeches during the crux of the play—this being the night the prostitute pours out her heart to a regular client, allows him to see what's really behind the façade she's presented to him for two years or more.

Be it drama, comedy or pantomime, it was great fun. All of it. Working behind the scenes was almost as much fun, too. That was how Charlotte had started: she had never envisaged herself acting, not even in an amateur capacity, and yet—yet it was a definite catharsis, a means of giving vent, of expressing herself, an artistry of which she was capable.

Unfortunately, Charlotte was in no other way artistic. Nobody regretted it more than she, for her love of the arts, almost all of them, ran deep. But she was not gifted herself, she couldn't paint, draw or write, and she had no musical ability. Discovering she could act, therefore, at least to a standard acceptable to the Park Lane Players, had come as a very pleasant surprise.

As she took the short ride home on the Tube, she cast her mind back to the argument she had put up when Geoffrey Hemmings had first asked her to attend one of the meetings, when the P.L.P. had been deciding on their next play. Geoffrey was on the committee, had invited her to come along and simply listen, see if she wouldn't perhaps consider helping them behind the scenes. And so she had. A couple of months later, when another play had been decided on, Charlotte had tried for the part of a maid, at Geoffrey's insistence, and she'd got it. And loved doing it!

Going back even further, Charlie hadn't wanted any involvement with Geoffrey to begin with. She had tried to avoid him. He lived immediately above her, in a one-bedroomed flat on the third floor of a smart building in a quiet road in West Kensington. Every morning for weeks on end, he had offered her a lift to work. That was when Charlie was temping and happened to work in the same street as Geoffrey. His offer stopped when her assignment changed, when they no longer found themselves leaving the building at precisely the same time. Then he found another way of talking to her—he simply rang her doorbell and asked her out. She declined. Time and again.

One day, sitting in the communal garden at the back of the building, the two of them had had their first real conversation and it was then that Geoffrey told her about his involvement with amateur dramatics. To this day there was nothing between them except friendship, though Charlie knew full well this was not what Geoffrey would have liked. The refusal to allow their friendship to develop into something more was on her part, and she was very firm about it. Only occasionally did she have dinner or lunch with him, usually when they both wanted, needed, a little extra time together to test their lines for the current play.

Geoffrey was nice enough, though. A sweet man, really. He was twenty-nine but he looked several years younger. He was also nice-looking and not short of girl-friends, when he made time for them, when he wanted to be bothered ... Charlie laughed at herself, she was being cynical again. She was, she had to admit, cynical about men in general—young ones, at any rate. She had been jilted once, didn't that explain it all? It was perhaps unfair in Geoffrey's case, he *did* take no for an answer, often! He was a trier, she had to say that much for him. In fact, there was more to him than met the eye, she'd discovered during the past two years. He gave the appearance of being shy, yet he was persistent in his quiet way. Looking at him, listening to him, one would never imagine him as an actor, albeit only with the local players.

All in all, their friendship was a nice arrangement. There had been occasions when Charlie had done a bit of sewing for Geoffrey, a button here, a trouser-hem there, in return for which he had put up an extra shelf in her kitchen and was more than willing to put plugs on things for her (which was something she knew *how* to do, but couldn't, for some reason). He owned his home, as did Charlotte. With help from her parents but mainly with the money she'd inherited from her grandmother, she had been able to buy the flat outright when she'd moved from the Lake District to London, when she'd begun to carve out a new and different life for herself, when . . .

She sighed, shaking herself out of her reverie as the train stopped at her station. Thinking back to the past was something she didn't care to do. She was a forward-thinking person, more concerned with the future than the past.

It was raining again, she discovered as she emerged on to the street.

It was still raining at eleven o'clock when she and Geoffrey were riding home in his car that night. They could have walked to the church hall where the P.L.P. rehearsed, but they hadn't. 'When's it going to stop?' she protested. 'I mean, what's happened to our summer?'

'We had that nice day in April . . .'

'Geoffrey, I'm serious. I'm sick of this weather!'

He took his eyes from the road, shooting a quick glance at her. 'You've been in a funny mood all evening. And it has nothing to do with the rotten weather.'

'Hey, just because I'm not word-perfect——'

'Nothing to do with that, either.' He brought the car to a halt in a parking space in the courtyard in front of their building. 'Something must have upset you at work today.'

'You're right.' What was the point in denying it? 'And no, before you ask, I don't want to talk about it. I've talked about it, and thought about it enough.'

'O.K., O.K.!' Geoffrey's dark hair glistened in the lamplight as he got out of the car. He came round and opened the door for her, always the gentleman. It was a little gesture she always appreciated, not being the type to accuse him of being a sexist pig and to tell him she was perfectly capable of opening her own door, thank you very much.

'Thanks.' She stood facing him, no taller, no shorter than he, thanks to the two-inch heels she had on. 'Sorry about the rehearsal, I know I shouldn't need the book at this stage——'

'Too right you shouldn't,' he teased. 'Are you inviting me in for coffee tonight?'

She smiled; she rarely did invite him in. Very rarely. There were boundaries which must not be crossed, he knew that. 'No, not tonight. I'm tired.'

He nodded his acceptance. 'O.K. Let me apologise again about lunch today. I——'

'There's no need, I understand.' He had already explained his non-appearance, pressure at work and all that. They walked up the first two flights of stairs to Charlie's front door, ignoring the lift, as usual.

'Can we make it tomorrow? Same time?'

'Why not?'

'Why not, indeed?' He smiled, with friendship, with admiration, without hope. 'Good night, Charlie.'

'Good night.' It was with relief that she let herself into her home. What she needed was a long soak in a hot bath. Perhaps that would return her spirits to normal. And who knew? Maybe the sun would shine tomorrow.

It did.

Tuesday began perfectly. Charlotte woke to find the sun streaming through the beige curtains at her bedroom window. She flung them open, smiled at the sky, showered and dressed and put on a little make-up in record time. Not that there was any hurry. She was in good spirits. Yesterday seemed aeons away. Yesterday was over and done with.

'Good morning, Linda!' She walked into the office ten minutes early, giggling because she'd greeted her secretary but her secretary hadn't arrived yet. So what? She was entitled to feel gay on such a beautiful morning, wasn't she? Who was to know if she had a belated case of spring fever? Life was good. Tonight's rehearsal would go perfectly! Lunch with Geoffrey would be pleasant. Yesterday's mishap would be sorted out in a jiffy, once and for all. All she had to do was pick up the phone, speak to the printer and hear his reassurance that the amendments to the proofs she'd given him were in hand, fully understood, in no danger of being overlooked . . .

At which point the door to the boss's office opened. 'Ah, Charlotte. I thought I heard you talking to someone?'

Charlie looked at him blankly. 'There's nobody here, Mr Grant.'

He shrugged, his expression worried. 'Janice isn't well.'

The smile faded from his assistant's face. 'I—I'm sorry to hear that.' She was, too. She dreaded to think how her boss would take it if——

'She keeps being sick in the morning,' he went on. 'I don't like it.'

'But—but Mr Grant!' How she prevented herself from laughing, she'd never know. 'Is that all? I mean, that's perfectly normal!'

'So she tells me, so I've heard, but it can't do the baby much good, can it? All that retching!'

The discussion, pointless though it was, went on for almost five minutes. Both bemused and amused, Charlie did a reassurance job on the sweet and kindly middle-aged man who was her boss. Bless him! She didn't know much about pregnancy herself, but really! She was relieved when Linda materialised and Mr Grant retreated into his own office.

He appeared again in the middle of the morning, different again. He'd spoken to his wife on the phone and all was well. Janice was normal again. Charlie only wished she could say the same for Edward. What was he going to be like when the baby was only weeks away, rather than months?

At noon she left the office, having been called into the gallery to sort out a problem. Forty minutes later she returned, had no sooner sat down at her desk than Mr Grant's door opened yet again. But this time it was Mr Maxwell who appeared. At least, it was he who emerged first. Mr Grant was hot on his heels.

Charlie's eyes shot immediately to Linda's, almost pleading, 'Why didn't you tell me?'

'I didn't have the chance!' came the silent reply.

And then, involuntarily, both girls' eyes were on those of the man whose presence dominated the room. Curtis Maxwell seemed impossibly tall, watched as he was by the seated Charlotte. She stood, quickly, every attitude of her body defensive as he planted himself firmly right by her desk. 'Good morning, Charlotte.'

'Mr Maxwell . . .' She wanted to look at her boss but was unable to take her eyes from the blue gaze that held her. She found herself unable to move at all. Linda, her fingers stationary over the keys of her typewriter, looked on in fascination. And Linda had been right. Curtis Maxwell was beautiful. On the outside. He was wearing a cream-coloured jacket with dark brown slacks and a very fine cotton polo-necked sweater of the same shade of brown. Tasteful. The colour combination suited him and though the clothes were casual, they were immaculate.

Charlotte observed all this although her eyes had not yet left his. Likewise she observed his features, the dark blond of his heavy eyebrows, the light blond of his hair, shot here and there with grey-white; the strong line of his jaw, the immovability it brought to mind . . . The straight nose, the unsmiling but no longer forbidding set of his mouth. But it was his eyes which caught and held the focus of her attention. They were as blue as the sky. Today's sky. A deep and definite blue. No longer cold and disapproving, they seemed so very different from the impression they had given yesterday . . .

'I believe I owe you an apology,' he began.

'I—not at all.'

'Oh, yes.' He released her for a moment, turning to glance at Edward. 'Your boss has explained. It seems you were not *au fait* with the instructions I gave Edward.'

'We-ll . . .' Charlotte had never felt so awkward in her life. 'Er—everything's sorted out, anyway.' She sat down again, needing to look elsewhere, needing to *do* something with a body which suddenly felt awkward, gauche. What the devil was wrong with her? And why didn't he clear off now he'd said his piece?

'I thought we'd have lunch together.' This was the answer to Charlotte's unspoken question. To say that it shocked her would be putting it mildly. She knew she hadn't misheard, yet she found herself responding as though she had.

'I beg your pardon?'

A smile flitted across his face, touching his eyes, doing magical things to them. It was gone as fast as it had appeared but it lasted long enough for her to realise he was laughing at her.

'Lunch, Charlotte.' The reiteration came from Mr Grant. 'Mr Maxwell wants to take you out to lunch.'

And don't you *dare* refuse! The unspoken instruction was very plain in her boss's tone—so plain that she didn't hesitate to answer. It was a gracious answer, spoken smilingly and with—apparently—the utmost sincerity. 'Why, that's very kind of you, Mr Maxwell. And I'd love to! But I'm afraid I have a date for lunch today.'

'You said that yesterday.'

It mightn't have been so difficult if there hadn't been an audience. But Linda was making no pretence at work, and as for Mr Grant—well! 'So I did.' She hadn't said it to *him*, but still. She was still smiling, though her self-consciousness had turned into embarrassment. 'And it was cancelled, if you remember. I—we fixed it for today instead.'

'So cancel it today.' Curtis Maxwell spoke as if she had overlooked the obvious. He had a nerve!

'I'm afraid I can't do that.' Her smile was becoming frozen, unnatural. She was aware if it. She was aware Mr Grant was aware of it. Oh, drat this man! He was playing games with her and while her boss was blissfully unaware of it, Charlie was not!

'There's no such thing as can't,' came the smooth reply. 'Not in my vocabulary.'

Charlotte's heart had begun to accelerate. Her embarrassment shifted to annoyance, acute annoyance. 'I'm afraid it's too late. Geoffrey will be on his way here by now. It's ten to one.'

'Geoffrey.' Just two syllables. How did he manage to pronounce them and at the same time give the impression that the person he spoke of was something that had just crawled out from under a stone?

'My—date. He'll already have left his office to come here.'

'Poor Geoffrey.' This time the name was said so politely, so lightly, that nobody noticed the sarcasm but Charlie. Before she could respond in any way, Curtis Maxwell had turned his back to her and was addressing her secretary. 'Do give Geoffrey Charlotte's apologies, Linda. I'm sure he'll understand.'

Linda nodded her obedience.

'Charlotte—if you're ready, then.' Oh, he wielded his power beautifully, she had to give him that! With the attitude of a beneficent uncle he inclined his head and offered her his arm. He did this with such slow and natural grace, she was left without any means of resistance. His choice of words, his delivery of them, trapped her into an inevitable response.

She stood and, as though they were far from strangers, took the proffered arm.

Charlie glanced at her grinning secretary, at her beaming boss who said, 'Don't hurry back, Charlotte. Enjoy your lunch.'

'I will,' she said pleasantly, her eyes returning to those of the man who towered by her side, shooting hazel-gold sparks of hatred at him.

He waited until they'd gone through the rooms of the gallery, until they'd reached the outside corridor, before he started laughing. Once started, he couldn't seem to stop.

Charlotte said not a word. Her only protest was an attempt to extract her arm from his. It didn't work. Not only did he react with the speed of lightning, his arm locking hers firmly in place, but it also added to his mirth.

The easiest thing to do was to let him laugh. What an obnoxious, arrogant, self-centred swine he was! Did he think himself clever? He had placed her in an impossible situation, knowing he had the power to get his own way, to win, and now he thought himself wonderful! Well, one thing was certain, he would never, ever, ask her to lunch again. She would treat this man with the contempt he deserved! Plainly and clearly. Oh, yes, she would be very clear about it.

Clear, but utterly, utterly charming with it.

After all, she didn't want to lose her job.

CHAPTER THREE

THEY came face to face with Geoffrey on the steps of the gallery. He stopped in his tracks, looking at Charlie and at Curtis Maxwell with a mixture of puzzlement and suspicion, his gaze taking in the proprietorial hold the other man had on her. She wanted desperately to wrench free of that hold, but she could hardly do that. And it wasn't simply the man's air of possessiveness that bothered her, it was the physical contact in itself. It was as though she had become hypersensitised where his body touched hers.

'Geoffrey, I—I'm sorry about this. I left a message with Linda and——' She broke off, remembering her manners. With her free arm, she gestured towards her captor. 'This is Mr Maxwell, Curtis Maxwell. Mr Maxwell, this is a friend of mine, Geoffrey Hemmings.'

Geoffrey was the first to acknowledge. 'How do you do?'

'Very nicely, thank you.' Curtis released his hold on Charlotte, only to let his arm slide to her waist, where it settled at the side as he propelled her down the steps. He glanced over his shoulder at the bewildered Geoffrey, throwing a blatantly false, 'So sorry about this, old chap! Business calls, you understand.' With a wave of his arm, he brought a taxi screeching to a halt and before Charlie could catch her breath, she was inside it.

Moving as far away from him as possible, she looked out of the window. She didn't dare speak, she was fuming so much she couldn't trust herself. Curtis didn't coax her, he made no attempt to take her arm again until they were getting out of the taxi. Two

minutes after that they were greeted by the head
waiter in a small French bistro and were shown to a
corner table with the comment, 'The table you asked
for, Mr Maxwell.'

Charlotte glanced around. The bistro was fairly
busy but conversations were subdued, the ambience
quiet and relaxed. They were in a small room which
led through archways into other small rooms, the walls
of which were painted white over rough plaster. The
shades of the wall lights were amber, as were the
candles on the tables. They were in a basement, there
were no windows at all, so of course all lights were lit,
the cutlery and glasses gleaming beneath them. The
place felt expensive.

Putting both hands flat against the smooth linen
tablecloth, Charlotte looked at her host and flashed
him her most brilliant smile. 'Well, this is all very
nice, Mr Maxwell, but what's it in aid of?'

She expected him to tie in this escapade with his
apology. But he didn't. He took his time about
answering her, letting his eyes linger on her mouth,
one eyebrow lifting slightly as her smile faded.
'What a pity, Charlotte. You're even more attractive
when you smile. You must have been told a hundred
times that . . .' As he went on, the drinks waiter
appeared, stood by their table with an impassive
face, pencil poised over pad. As far as Curtis was
concerned, there was no one else present. '. . . your
eyes can only be described as fabulous. You're an
extremely attractive woman, and that's all the
justification I need to invite you out to lunch,
wouldn't you agree?'

Awkwardly aware of the listening waiter, she
couldn't answer Curtis in any vein. 'I'll—have a
Campari-soda, please.'

'Make it two. Don't put any ice in mine.'

He watched her, smiling, when they were alone
again. 'Are you giving me the silent treatment, then?

Firstly in the taxi and now in here—is this how I'm to be rewarded after all the trouble I've gone to?'

'Trouble?' she blurted. What was he talking about? And what had happened to her behaviour plan? He'd so disconcerted her with his answer to her first question, she wasn't thinking straight. She wasn't thinking straight because she could have sworn he really meant what he'd said.

'I cancelled two appointments for this, got to your office around twelve in order to be sure of catching you in time.'

'I—can't imagine why.'

'Can't you?' His mouth wasn't smiling but his eyes were laughing at her. 'Why do you have to be told everything twice, Charlotte? Why do you behave as if you have the IQ of a donkey, when I know full well you're an intelligent woman? You spent three years working for an arts degree—oh, yes, I had quite a chat about you with Edward—so you can't possibly be as slow as you're making yourself out to be.'

Again she couldn't answer him. For one thing, another waiter arrived with menus, for another she was wound up so tightly inside, she couldn't relax enough to talk. Because he was so damn good to look at, she found herself trying to avoid doing so; because he was flirting with her, she had become suspicious. She had planned to treat him with contempt, contempt beneath a veneer of charm. But she didn't, it seemed, have the necessary sophistication. Not with the likes of him.

'Mr Maxwell——' she began at length, after he'd given their orders.

'Curtis.'

Charlie began again. 'Mr Maxwell, I'm aware of your importance, your generosity to the art school, which in turns means our gallery——'

'Forget all that.' He seemed displeased. 'Why don't you just relax and be yourself?'

'But that's just it! How can I, in the circumstances?'

'There are no "circumstances", except that you and I got off to a most unfortunate start. I'm trying to rectify that, Charlotte. I'm attracted to you, I'd like to see more of you, I'd like to know you better. How many times,' he finished softly, his smile slow and easy, 'do I have to tell you?'

If she'd been nervous before, she was doubly nervous now. She lapsed for a few minutes into small talk, saying something inane about the bistro and its décor. He was altogether too smooth, altogether too attractive. And he knew it. She couldn't handle his charm, couldn't reconcile him with the man she had met only yesterday, couldn't handle his—his honesty!

It got worse. As she realised how she must sound, babbling rather, to her horror she found herself blushing, and making matters worse by trying frantically to cover it and saying something about the food which had just been placed in front of her. 'This—this looks good. *Bon appetit*, Mr Maxwell.'

Mr Maxwell—so that's how it was. Curtis liked a challenge, liked nothing better, in fact. Smiling both to himself and to her, he inclined his head slightly and decided to take a different tack.

By the time they were half-way through the next course, they were deep into a discussion about Van Gogh and his madness. By the time they'd finished their heaped plates of fresh strawberries with cream, they were talking about Renoir and his attitude to women. When coffee arrived, Curtis reluctantly had to steal a glance at his watch. 'Hell, I have to go.'

Charlotte blinked. 'What time is it?'

'Ten past three.'

'Ten—heavens, I'll get the sack!'

'Hardly! No, stay right where you are. Nothing's so desperate that we can't finish our coffee. I can't imagine anything more uncivilised than having a splendid lunch which isn't rounded off by a good, strong cup of coffee. Can you?'

He spoke the last two words so seriously, Charlie couldn't help laughing. 'No.' She answered with all the drama she was capable of. 'That would be dreadful!'

'You're sending me up.' He was laughing, too.

'How right you are!'

'You know,' he went on, leaning back in his seat to survey her, 'there's something else I dislike intensely.'

Charlotte raised delicately arched brows slowly, her eyes sparkling. 'Do go on.' She heard the softness in her voice, the teasing in it. Was it the wine or was it the company? Or was it both? How had he seduced her so, firstly into a serious discussion, then into laughter, and now—now she was almost flirting with the man!

'Having to break off an interesting conversation, most especially when it's with an attractive woman. Let's finish it over dinner tonight. Shall we say eight o'clock?'

She came down to earth rapidly. Trying to resent his presumption—shall we say eight o'clock, indeed!—didn't work. Something had happened during the two hours she'd been in his company, she had stopped disliking him. What at first she had seen as arrogance she now thought of as self-assurance. Who could resent that in a person, provided it wasn't overdone? On the contrary, it was enviable. None the less, she put together as many mental barriers against him as she could. It wasn't difficult, she had only to remember the way he spent his weekends. Well, he was entitled to, of course, but if he amused himself in town with other women during the week, she wasn't going to be one of them. In any case, she had the perfect reason for a polite refusal. 'I can't, I'm otherwise committed.'

'Geoffrey?'

'No.' Well, not exactly!

'You realise he's in love with you?'

'I realise no such thing!'

'But you know he wants you?'

Charlotte's eyes widened. There were times when this man got right to the point, she'd learned that much about him! 'That's hardly the same thing.'

'I didn't mean to imply that it was. In Geoffrey's case however, it's both.'

'And it's none of your business, Curtis!'

He registered the use of his first name, her first usage of it. She didn't. 'True,' he conceded. 'Now where were we? Ah, yes, about tomorrow——'

'I can't have dinner with you tomorrow, either. Or Thursday.'

'Can't or won't?'

'Both. To put it plainly,' she said with no attempt at charm, 'I don't want to.'

The smile he gave her then brought her eyes immediately to his mouth. He smiled fully, genuinely amused by her. 'If there's one thing I find uninteresting, it's a woman who just can't say no to a man. Where's the fun in that?'

How could she not laugh at that? She couldn't. She tried, but laughter came bubbling from her of its own accord. 'I'll come clean with you, Mr Maxwell——'

'It was Curtis a moment ago.'

'Was it really?' She put on an exaggerated frown. 'How very remiss of me! As I was saying, I'm not interested—in you or in any other man. No, don't look at me like that, I'm a perfectly normal human being. I just—don't need that scene. Not at the moment.'

The lack of inflection in his reply only added to its ambiguity. 'Possibly an enviable position to be in, Charlotte. For myself, I have to say I need a great deal of it. Like Renoir, I happen to adore women. However, unlike him, I never idealise them.'

Charlotte tried to put a stop to the conversation then. 'For a man who's in a hurry, you're lingering rather.'

'That's because I'm enchanted by you, Charlotte.'
Again there was no inflection. 'Now then, what *are*
you doing tonight, tomorrow and Thursday?'

'I'm rehearsing for a play. I'm a member of——'

'Ah, yes, amateur dramatics. I heard you mention it
to my temporary secretary, whatshername.'

'Margaret. How much of that conversation did you
hear?' she asked casually.

'Just the tail end. The bit about Geoffrey and the
amateur dramatics. Why? Did I miss something?'

Relieved, Charlie avoided that one. 'You were
eavesdropping, deliberately!'

'My dear girl, by definition eavesdropping is
deliberate. I do it whenever I get the chance.' He
signalled for the bill. 'So what play are you doing?'

'It's called *Count your Regrets at Midnight.*'

'I've never heard of it. It sounds heavy.'

'It is and it isn't. It's rather an obscure piece. It has
its amusing moments and there is a moral to it.'

'I like a story with a moral. So when does it hit the
stage?'

His choice of words had her laughing again. 'It *hits*
the local church hall in a couple of weeks—hence the
extra rehearsal night.'

'Which nights do you rehearse?'

She told him they normally rehearsed Tuesday,
Wednesday and Thursday, but that at the moment,
they worked Mondays, too. Friday wasn't mentioned
by either of them. Fridays he left town, did he not?

At his assurance that he was heading in the same
direction, Charlie accepted the lift back to work by
taxi. She thanked him warmly for lunch, and she
meant it. She hadn't realised until this moment quite
how much she'd enjoyed it. In fact if she were honest
with herself, she felt loath to leave him now. They
were standing by the taxi, the hum of its engine, the
click of its meter the background to their goodbyes.

'You realise,' Curtis said, 'that you managed to get

through all that time without telling me anything about yourself?'

'But you learned a great deal about me.'

He laughed, amused by her differentiation. 'I'll grant you that. But tell me something mundane, satisfy my curiosity about what I heard in your voice—where do you hail from?'

'The Lake District.'

'Lucky you. And lucky me. As it happens, I'm driving up there for the weekend.'

The name Chris was in her head again. It would make a change from the Cotswolds, she supposed. 'As it happens,' she said without thinking, 'so am I.'

His interest was apparent. 'When are you leaving?'

'Friday. I'm taking the day off, have to be at a wedding on Saturday morning, an old school-friend——'

'And when do you plan to come back?'

'Sunday, of course. I have to be at work on Monday, not to mention the rehearsal . . .'

He was still smiling at her, the meter was still ticking, time was marching on for both of them. He had an appointment to get to and she was ridiculously late back to the office.

'I'm coming back on Sunday, too. Alas, mine is a business trip. Well, primarily, though I'm staying with someone I can call a friend. He's an art collector, an old and valued customer who lives just outside Kendal. You'll be staying with your parents, I take it?'

Charlotte nodded.

'And where in the Lake District do they live?'

Charlotte found herself unwilling to answer that one. 'Kendal,' she said dully. Her mind was racing: he'd said he was driving up, he might offer her a lift, and that was the last thing she wanted. No, no he would hardly do that when he wouldn't be travelling alone.

Nor did he.

CHAPTER FOUR

THE message came not the next day but the day after. Via Mr Grant. To be precise, it was delivered more as an itinerary than as a message, a *fait accompli*. It was another example of Curtis Maxwell's capacity for presumption, and Charlie resented it, schooling her features into a smile and fuming silently as her boss repeated what he thought was good news for her.

She had been called into his office specifically. It was five minutes past nine on Thursday morning. Charlotte had arrived at nine on the dot, Mr Grant, presumably, had arrived at his usual eight-thirty, since he had had the call from Curtis 'some twenty minutes ago'.

'He said he'll collect you from your flat at nine in the morning,' Mr Grant was saying. 'Nice of him, isn't it? Although I suppose it was the obvious thing to do, since you both happen to be going to Kendal this weekend. Still——'

'Very nice of him,' Charlotte agreed stiffly. And flaming audacious, too! How dared he make this suggestion through her boss? How dared he not speak directly to her? Most of all, how *dared* he think that just because Chris had declined the trip—which she must have—he might just as well have her company instead?

'He said there was no point in taking two cars. Of course I told him you haven't got a car, and to that he said——'

'I'm afraid I have other plans for the journey.'

'You have? Oh, dear, that *is* unfortunate!'

'Why?' she almost snapped at him.

'Because I'm not sure you'll be able to reach him

47

now. He said he was just leaving town for the day . . .
Oh, this is unfortunate! If you'd only mentioned to
me—I had no idea—I take it someone else is giving
you a lift?'

What could she say to that? Yes, British Rail?
Hardly! It wasn't as if she'd bought her ticket, even.
Drat the man! With an effort, she put on another
smile. Mr Grant was managing to take this personally,
somehow. Or he was afraid of offending Curtis. Or
both. It was all getting out of hand. 'Not to worry, I'll
sort something out. If I can't reach Mr Maxwell, I'll
change my plans and be ready when he calls at nine
tomorrow.'

Her boss looked enormously relieved. She did not
go on to tell him that she would reach Curtis Maxwell
by hook or by crook. If he wasn't in his office now, she
would find out from Maggie where he was. No
problem.

But there was a problem. Maggie didn't know where
he was. 'But—but you said he always tells you his
movements!'

'Sure, but only when he wants me to know, only when
he decides to be available. I don't know where he is every
minute of every day. Grief, what's the problem? It has to
be major, you are one very uptight lady!'

Was that how she sounded? 'No, no, it's just—it's
nothing. Well, something and nothing.' And with that,
she bade Margaret goodbye. There was no way she
was going to put her in the picture. Maggie would get
well and truly carried away with all sorts of wrong
ideas!

There was, she told herself, still no problem. If he
couldn't be reached today, he could be reached this
evening, tonight, she would ring him at midnight, if
necessary. He lived in London, didn't he? If he didn't
live in that flat above the Mayfair gallery, he couldn't
be too far away. There were, after all, such things as
telephone directories.

Which was true. But Curtis Maxwell wasn't listed.

On getting home from work, before dashing off to rehearsal, Charlotte hastily ate a sandwich while poring over the telephone directory. There was nothing there except the addresses and numbers of Curtis's galleries. In vain she tried five numbers listed as C. Maxwell; none of them belonged to him.

At ten thirty that evening, immediately on getting home from the church hall, she tried directory enquiries. 'Yes,' she was told, 'we have a listing for Curtis Maxwell.'

'At the address of the Maxwell Gallery in Mayfair?' Charlie ventured.

'Yes, that's correct.'

'Super! That's the number I'm after.'

'I'm afraid I can't give you the number.'

'What?'

'I said——'

'But *why*?' she demanded, even as she realised what the answer would be.

It was ex-directory.

She sat cross-legged on the floor, staring at the telephone and feeling trapped. She was trapped. She might just as well get on with her packing.

Friday was another nice day, she hoped Saturday would be the same for the sake of Felicity who was getting married in the morning. Stepping out of the shower at a little after seven, Charlie set about the task of blow-drying her heavy russet mane. By a quarter to nine she was ready and waiting, moving around the living-room of her flat because she couldn't sit still.

Telling herself she was behaving irrationally, she tried to analyse why this was. She thought again, inevitably, of the 'little lady' in the Cotswolds, as Maggie had referred to her. But she, Charlotte, was not supposed to know about that, so she ought not to let it affect her behaviour towards Curtis. But how could she not? What *did* the man want of her?

Then again, perhaps there was nothing more to his offering her this lift than the logic her boss had seen in the gesture. But then ... face it, she told herself, he's been on your mind ever since you had lunch with him on Tuesday. Face it, you don't want to spend hours in a car alone with him. It was a long haul from London to Kendal, five or six hours by road, according to her father, who made the trip from time to time.

When the doorbell rang she tried to calm herself, to put all this into perspective and to behave civilly. For the sake of good manners, if nothing else, it would not be right to greet him with the statement that she hadn't wanted this lift.

'Good morning, Mr Maxwell.' Even as she spoke, her eyes moved of their own volition over all the features of his face, sweeping downwards to observe the pale blue of a shirt which was open at the neck, its sleeves rolled back to the elbow, white slacks, white socks and soft leather shoes, also white.

Curtis responded similarly, his eyebrows lifting ever so slightly as he took in the outline of her figure under the rose-pink cotton shift she was wearing. 'It is now. You're in the wrong business, you should have been a model. You look fabulous, such a simple little dress, but what the body does for it——'

'I'm ready if you are.'

'Aren't you going to invite me in?'

There was her suitcase to pick up. Stepping backwards, she gestured him into the living-room, where he stood, looking round, nodding his approval. 'Very nice, Charlotte, tasteful simplicity. I like your choice of décor, the feeling for colours——' Abruptly he stopped, taking her by surprise by turning suddenly, catching her chin in the palm of a hand. 'What's the matter?'

'I—nothing.' Except that her heart had started leaping about, except for the sudden, tingling warmth where his hand touched her skin. Again she stepped away from him. 'My case is over there.'

There was a bark of laughter. 'That's your packing for the weekend? I'd have said you were going away for a month!'

He had her laughing again. How did he do it? 'I've got a wedding to attend, remember? I've only packed the bare essentials——'

'That's what they all say!'

Her laughter faded at that. No doubt he knew women and their habits very well indeed.

'Hey, I'm joking. It makes no difference, there's bags of room in the boot.'

The boot was that of a Jaguar, navy-blue and gleaming in the morning sun. Charlotte was helped into the passenger seat and reminded to fasten her safety-belt. Settling back into the plush leather comfort, she tried again to quell her inexplicable nervousness. She failed. When Curtis got in beside her she found herself, as she had known she would, acutely aware of his nearness; she found the very size of him attractive, the width of his shoulders, the depth of his chest, the tautness of his body which was in peak condition.

She was, she realised miserably, extremely attracted to him physically. As he was to her. He'd told her as much.

Danger!

She felt she was in danger. She had never experienced this before, an attraction of this strength. Looking at him was becoming compulsive. The confines of the car were too—intimate, she had to drag her eyes away from him as they set off, away from the hard muscles of his forearms, away from the solid strength of his thighs, made all the more fascinating by the way his slacks were pulled tightly over them now he was seated.

They drove in silence for a while, Charlotte looking

determinedly out of the window at a landscape which was as yet uninteresting and all too familiar.

'Now, where were we?' Curtis broke the silence. 'Oh, yes, I asked you what was wrong but you didn't get round to telling me.'

'I told you—nothing,' she said pleasantly.

He made no comment, he simply pressed his left indicator, negotiated his way into the left-hand lane and drew the car to a halt. With the attitude of a headmaster to an errant pupil, he told her, 'Now then, Charlotte, we have a long journey ahead of us and I don't like the vibes you're giving off. Not all of them, anyhow,' he added with a grin. 'So why don't you make the protests you're longing to make and clear the air?'

'So you're a mind-reader as well as presumptuous, about *the* most presumptuous person I've ever met. Why didn't you offer me a lift on Tuesday? When we spoke about going to Kendal then?' She had raised her brows in challenge. Let him answer that!

'Because you would have refused,' he said reasonably, as though it were the most obvious thing in the world. 'I had to arrange things the way I did to be sure of having the pleasure of your company today.'

She stared at him. Did he have an answer to everything? Did he know her that well—already? 'I tried to ring you last night, to put you off.'

'I thought you might. My private flat is ex-directory.'

'So I learned! Look, Mr Maxwell——'

'Stop it, Charlotte!' He was both irritated and amused. 'Stop it, you're fighting a losing battle.'

'What—I don't know what you mean.' The engine was running, people were tooting at them, obliged to drive around the parked car in the flow of Friday morning traffic. 'We'd better move on.'

'When I'm good and ready. When you have been made to realise that all we're doing is taking a drive together. There's no need to feel threatened, I'm not about to assault you. You are in no danger. Now, do you see that?'

Charlie felt very small in that moment, she felt small and childish and idiotic. Heavens, she wasn't frightened of men, not in the least! So why was she behaving as though she were? She pulled herself together smartly. 'You're right, Mr Maxwell, and I'm sorry.'

'Curtis.'

She gave up, once and for all. 'Curtis.'

They drove on, she wondering what he'd meant by 'a losing battle', he privately reassessing her for the umpteenth time.

'So tell me about this wedding you're going to,' Curtis said at length. 'An old schoolfriend, you said?'

'That's right.' Glad of the change of subject, Charlotte began to talk freely, finding herself relaxing fully as she did so. 'Well, actually, Felicity is the sister of a friend, though we all went to the same school. She, I mean her sister Joanne, was killed, riding on the pillion seat of a motorbike, when she was twenty.'

They glanced at one another, their eyes silently remarking on the tragedy of it. 'That's one reason I'm going back for this wedding, in a way I feel I'll be taking Joanne's place. Oh, Felicity has her full complement of bridesmaids, people she sees every day, but still . . .

'I left home shortly after Joanne's death,' she went on. 'I was twenty-one and obliged to have a re-think about my future. I'd finished my three years at the poly, another close girl friend had just got married, Joanne was dead and—it didn't seem there was any reason for me to stay in Kendal, much as I love it. Much as I love the Lake District. Job prospects were better for me in London.'

'Obliged to have a rethink?' Curtis repeated. 'What have you omitted to mention?'

Charlotte's smile was a gentle one, the look she stole at him tinged with admiration. This man didn't miss anything. Nothing at all! 'That I was also engaged at that point. I had been since I was seventeen.'

'Since before you left for college?'

'Since before I left for college. I see you've got the picture.'

'You went home to find you were no longer in love with him?'

'Almost right.' This time her smile was rueful. 'It was the other way round. Dennis and I had seen each other in the holidays, naturally. Our relationship had never been what I could describe as exciting. I'd known him all my life—boy-next-door sort of thing. But it was a comfortable one, secure, I thought, a good foundation for marriage. No, everything worked out for the best. He discovered what it was like to be in love. But not with me. He never was in love with me, any more than I was in love with him.'

'So you're not complaining?'

'I'm grateful!'

'Now,' he mused, 'since you said that with such vehemence, am I to take it you've become anti-marriage?'

'No. If it happens, it happens. All in good time. In the mean time, I'm happy. I'll just wait and see.'

'Bit of a fatalist, eh?'

'I'm young,' she countered.

Curtis took his eyes from the road just long enough to let her see a wry smile. 'Do I have to ask or are you going to volunteer?'

'Twenty-three,' she laughed. 'I'll be twenty-four in August.' She paused. 'And you?'

'Thirty-six. Thirty-seven in November.'

'I didn't mean that, actually. I meant, are you happy?'

'Fair to middling.' There was an almost imperceptible edge to his voice. Almost.

Charlotte read it as a barrier and ignored it. 'Is that all? And what of your own attitude to marriage? How come you've reached such a grand old age and escaped?'

His laughter was a low rumble. 'Thanks very much!'

She waited. And waited. 'You haven't answered my question, Curtis.'

She was obliged to wait again. It was only for seconds, but they were meaningful, telling seconds. 'I'll never marry.' The words came crisply, making it clear that she had gone far enough. 'I have a lot of commitments in my life as it is.'

Charlotte immediately began to talk on, about Kendal, about herself. She told him she was an only child, that her father had an antique shop where her mother occasionally helped out. But all the time she was talking, she was wondering. How strangely those words had been spoken, 'I'll never marry.' And how carefully he had considered whether or not he should say them at all. She felt, inexplicably but for certain, that in some way she should feel complimented that he had told her this.

It was some time later that she asked him why he was pulling off the motorway. 'Lunch, of course! I hope you're in agreement.'

'Definitely! But there are no services here.'

'Oh, I think we can do better than that, don't you? Not that I know where I'm going,' he added laughingly as they approached a roundabout. 'But we'll find somewhere suitable.'

They had lunch in a comfy, country pub which offered an array of hot and cold dishes. It was while they were eating that Charlotte asked him about *The Lady in White*. She did so cautiously, and she was right to be cautious. While she didn't feel it as strongly as she had earlier, she was aware of certain barriers in him.

'May I ask you, Curtis, because I'm simply dying

to!' she began lightly. 'It is true that *The Lady in White* is your mother?'

'Edward told you?'

'Yes.'

'What else did he tell you?'

'Nothing.'

'About me, I mean.'

'Nothing, honestly, nothing at all.'

'It's true.'

'Then your family knew Fernando Licer.'

He glanced around, possibly an unconscious gesture, as if to make sure they weren't overheard. 'We all knew him.'

Charlie's eyebrows went up. 'You, too?'

'I was eleven when he died.'

And that was as far as she dared go. His attitude, his tone told her that, although he had spoken casually, had even been smiling. But the smile hadn't reached his eyes.

'Well!' She shook her head as if to clear it of all the questions she wanted to ask. 'What are we having for pudding?'

Curtis's eyes travelled slowly, appreciatively, over the length of her body. 'I've had enough. You go ahead.'

'*I* can afford to.'

'You're very cheeky. Wait till you turn thirty, you won't find it so easy to keep such a perfect figure.'

'Perfect? If only you knew how I'd love to put on some weight!'

'You're crazy!' His eyes were on her breasts, braless beneath the cotton covering. 'I wouldn't change a thing about you, Charlotte.'

'One man's meat.'

He countered that with a very softly spoken, 'Whatever turns you on.'

She got to her feet before her blush took over, heading for the bar and its array of goodies.

They emerged from the pub to find that the day had grown even hotter. Once inside the Jaguar, Curtis touched a button and the sunroof opened, allowing the light and a welcome breeze to stream in as he set the car in motion.

Within the hour, Charlie was asleep.

She woke up in three stages. Firstly she became aware that something was missing. Too still. Too quiet. Then her eyes closed even more tightly against a bright light. She stirred, mumbled something unintelligible, provoking soft laughter from the man who was watching her.

Opening her eyes for a second, she registered that Curtis was watching her with the appreciation of a hungry man at a feast. His eyes were moving rapidly from her tumble of hair and back to her face, to every feature of it. As she squinted, he obligingly leaned over her, casting a shadow over her face, cutting off the sun.

Charlotte snapped fully awake, realising they were in a lay-by, that there was no traffic flashing past, that there were trees all around them.

She heard the quietly spoken, 'Gorgeous. Absolutely gorgeous,' and froze, her eyes drawn immediately to his. Her head was resting against the back of the seat, which was reclined slightly, and she didn't move a muscle, was locked in the warmth of the blue gaze which at once excited and alarmed her, bringing her eyes wide open. She could see what was coming, she could see it in his eyes, and her mind shouted in protest. Don't! Please don't!

'I'm not going to.' Curtis was so close she could feel the breeze of his breath on her cheek. She hadn't thought aloud, she knew she hadn't, yet there it was again, 'I'm not going to kiss you, Charlotte. Because if I do, I might never stop.'

'Curtis——'

'It's been a long time since I've wanted a woman the

way I want you.' His voice caressed her, his eyes
brilliant with the intensity of what he was saying. 'I
want you very much. I'd like to lay you down gently
on satin sheets and——'

This time she spoke his name with a protest. A
finger covered her lips. 'And undress you slowly, very
slowly, discovering——'

'Stop it!' She pushed his hand away, pulling herself
upright, unable to believe what he was doing to her.
She had been half mesmerised by him, by the mental
images he'd conjured for her. Worse, she was *aroused*!
'You're the one who's crazy!'

'Oh, I could be.' His voice hadn't changed one iota.
'I very easily could be, Charlotte.'

'What—why have we stopped?' Her fingers were in
her hair, trying to push it into some semblance of
order.

Curtis took one lingering look at what she was doing
before pulling away and putting both hands very
firmly on the wheel. 'We're just outside Kendal. I
need your directions from here.'

'Right.' She tried to be brisk, with the result that
she almost snapped at him. 'Er——' She looked
around, getting her bearings. 'Carry on, I'll direct you
when we're nearer town.'

Dear God, what had she let herself in for? Time and
again, as she directed him towards her parents' house,
she glanced at him surreptitiously. He fascinated her,
there were no two ways about it. Fascinated and
attracted her more than anyone she had ever met in
her life. It was a long time before her heart levelled off
to a steady beat. It was a long time before she could
cease her battle for control. Mind over body.

When he drew to a halt outside her parents' house,
Charlotte's heart reacted again. This time, it sank. She
had hoped she might get out of the car, see him on his
way before her mother spotted her. But it was too late.
Waving and smiling, Pauline Graham was already

half-way down the drive, signalling to this total
stranger that he should park the car there.

Curtis responded at once, slowing the car to a crawl
as it, and Pauline, moved towards the house. 'Good
afternoon! Mrs Graham, I take it? With that glorious
hair, you have to be Charlotte's mother!'

Charlie groaned inwardly. In the face of such
charm, she knew very well how her mother would
react. In any case, no matter who had delivered her
daughter to her door, Pauline would not have let them
leave without at least a cup of tea and something she
had baked that day.

With modern, youthful parents (they were in their
late forties), whose outlook on life was optimistic and
easygoing, Charlie knew she should count herself
lucky. And so she did. It was just that—that what?
Something, somehow, was trying to tell her that this
weekend was not going to unfold as she had imagined.

Nor did it. No sooner were all the introductions
and explanations completed than Charlotte's father
came home. It was four-thirty, the time she had
estimated she would get there. More introductions,
explanations.

'Well, it's very good of you, Mr Maxwell!' Eric
Graham sat in the armchair he always sat in and
gestured for his guest to be seated. Pauline had already
gone to put the kettle on, having whisked Charlotte's
suitcase away at the same time.

'Curtis.'

'Curtis. How long did the drive take? Usually takes
me between five and six hours.'

'Ah, well, we had a rather leisurely lunch.'

Eric's eyes twinkled as he surveyed his daughter.
'I'll bet. Eats like a horse, our Charlotte, and never
puts on an ounce.'

'I think she eats very daintily, Eric.'

Charlie looked from one man to the other, unable to
prevent herself from joining in their laughter.

'You come to London now and then?' asked Curtis. 'On business, I suppose?'

'Yes. I like to look round the antique fairs and whatnot.'

'Of course, you're in the business. Charlotte did tell me. Maybe you know the chap I'm staying with? He's fond of antiques, he lives about half-way between here and Windermere, Sir Kevin——'

'Loxley! Loxley Hall. I know him well, I've known him for years. He's one of my best customers. He has a penchant for antique silver, among other things. Paintings for one. He's known Charlotte since she was a little girl. Isn't that right, dear?'

'Yes.' It was true enough, not that she knew Sir Kevin well. Everyone around here knew him slightly, at least, or of him, at the very least. 'Daddy, Curtis is Curtis Maxwell of the Maxwell Galleries.'

Eric Graham tapped himself on the forehead. 'Of course! I should have realised straight away.'

Charlie extracted herself and went to unpack. She was anxious to hang up the white suit she was wearing to the wedding tomorrow. When she went back to the living-room, everything was as she could have predicted. Her father and Curtis were into a discussion about antiques and paintings, her mother was giving them tea and home-made scones . . . and biscuits . . . and cakes . . .

An hour passed. A fresh pot of tea appeared. Another half-hour passed, then Curtis looked at his watch, startled. 'Dear me! Forgive me, but I must— Pauline, would you mind if I use your phone?'

'Not at all!'

Charlotte suppressed a smile. Mind? Her mother would have made this man a gift of it!

'There's an extension in the kitchen, Curtis, if you want privacy.'

'No, no, I'll speak from here, that's O.K.'

And so they were all present when Curtis phoned

his mistress.

Automatically Charlotte had assumed he was calling Sir Kevin to explain his delay in getting to Loxley Hall. Wrong! Instead she was obliged to stay where she was, a polite smile on her face while all conversations halted and she heard,

'Chris? Hello, lovely! Thank goodness I caught you before six. I wanted to wish you good luck tonight. I know you'll cope beautifully . . . Yes, all's well with me. See you soon. 'Bye.'

That was all there was to it. More than enough to resurrect a whole host of resentment in Charlotte. And then some! 'Perhaps you'd better be on your way, Curtis,' she heard herself saying.

At the look she got from both parents, at the sudden silence, she added awkwardly, 'I mean—isn't Sir Kevin expecting you in time for dinner?'

'You're right,' Curtis responded smoothly, easing her parents out of their discomfort as he got to his feet and stretched. His attitude had been and still was that of a man who was in familiar surroundings, an old friend of the family. Only his gracious thanks and farewell to her parents indicated otherwise.

'It's been lovely.' Pauline was on her feet. So was Eric.

Charlie remained seated. Her heart was thumping yet again—this time in *anger*.

'But we'll see you on Sunday, when you collect Charlotte,' said her father. Then, a warning note in his voice, 'Charlotte? Curtis is leaving now.'

Get up and see him out, in other words. You have not been brought up to behave like this!

Dutifully, she escorted Curtis to the front door. He seemed unaware that anything was amiss with her. She was wrong about that, too.

'You certainly blow hot and cold,' he told her as she opened the door. 'What now? Did I overstay my welcome? Your parents——'

'Are enchanted.' She smiled. She was *not* going to
tell him what was upsetting her. She was damned if
she would! 'It's just—I'm a little tired, need to take a
rest.'

One eyebrow rose sardonically. 'After the three-
hour sleep you had in the car? If you say so, Charlotte.
'Bye for now.' And with that, to her intense
annoyance, he stooped and planted a kiss on the tip of
her nose.

Pauline Graham did not question her daughter that
evening, curious though she was. Curtis was mentioned
over dinner, naturally, but no questions were asked.
But they were there. So Charlotte gave her parents a
full, if edited, version of her short acquaintance with
him. 'And I must say, he seems very pleasant,' she
finished.

'Very.' There was a twinkle in her mother's eye.
'Not to mention handsome.'

Eric agreed with that, though that's as far as it went
with him. There was no twinkle in his eye.

After dinner, Charlotte took herself off to Felicity's
house. She got home around eleven to find both
parents in bed, all lights off except that of the hall.
They were both the early-to-bed, early-to-rise type.

It was during the following afternoon that Charlotte
found herself giving away more than she'd intended.
She got back from the wedding luncheon around three
o'clock and started to tell her mother about it as soon
as she got through the door. The bride had been
beautiful, how kind the weather was and——

'Sir Kevin phoned!' Pauline didn't try to hide her
pleasure.

Charlotte flung herself on to the settee, knowing
something ominous was happening. 'And?'

And he had had quite a chat with Pauline. Talked
about Curtis, about Charlotte. If only he had realised
that Curtis and Charlotte were friends! Dinner tonight
at Loxley Hall—just a small dinner party. Bit of a

liberty to rob Pauline of her daughter's company when he knew she didn't see her often. She didn't mind too much? Curtis would be delighted. And so would he. Always had a soft spot for little Charlotte. What a chatterbox she used to be when she was younger! Would send his chauffeur with the car at seven.

There was, Charlotte realised after two minutes of arguing, no point in arguing. Pauline was delighted, Sir Kevin was a very good customer of her father. It would be lovely to dine at Loxley Hall. And if Pauline were younger, 'believe you me,' she'd jump at the chance of having dinner with Curtis Maxwell.

The anger inside Charlotte doubled. 'I'll go, Mummy, but there's something I think you'd better understand. I am not interested in Curtis. Yes, he's attractive, yes, he can be charming. But that's it. You remember that call he made yesterday? To someone called Chris? Well, for your information, that's his mistress. From what I can gather, she lives in the Cotswolds and he services her every, or nearly every, weekend.'

'*Charlotte!* What an expression!'

'I'm sorry, but its accurate.'

'It isn't like you to be——'

'Vulgar. I know, I've said I'm sorry, but that's how I see it.'

'But—but who's told you this?'

Charlie duly put her mother in the picture as far as Maggie was concerned.

'But you—she—might have the wrong end of the stick!'

'Not a chance!'

Pauline looked dubious, then her face softened into a smile. 'Darling, how young you are! How black and white the ways of the world, in your eyes. You know what they say about face value. You *could* be wrong.'

In a pig's eye. Charlie didn't say it; she'd given up. 'Now *what* am I going to wear, for heaven's sake?'

'What's wrong with what you're wearing?'

The younger woman looked down at the white suit she'd worn to the wedding. It was a dressy sort of suit, true, embroidered on the collar, again with white. And there wasn't a mark on it, but, 'It's crumpled. I'd need a fresh blouse. I——'

'No problem. Take it off, I'll sponge and press it. And it just so happens I have the perfect blouse you can wear.'

'Mother, you're two sizes smaller than I am.'

'It isn't mine. It's a present for Pam, for her birthday next week. I'll replace it with something else. Now stop sulking, Charlotte, it isn't like you.'

She was still sulking, inwardly, when Sir Kevin's car rolled up at seven on the dot.

CHAPTER FIVE

CHARLOTTE might have enjoyed herself had it not been for her anger with Curtis. Had it not been for Pippa Loxley.

Sir Kevin, an elderly widower, had introduced Pippa as his niece, a 'favourite' who had descended on him unannounced for the weekend. In her early thirties, she was tall, elegant, beautiful and, Charlie learned during the course of the evening, recently divorced.

Regardless of her anger, Charlie found it an interesting evening one way and another. During cocktails and later throughout dinner she coped beautifully, unaccustomed though she was to such splendid surroundings and to being waited on in a private house by staff. Sir Kevin's 'small' dinner party consisted of fourteen people. Presiding at the head of the table, he had seated her to his left, his niece was opposite and sitting next to Curtis. Why wasn't she, Charlie, next to Curtis? Had Pippa asked to be put next to him? Probably. She had already told the younger girl that she and Curtis had 'got to know one another' during the day. Also there had been, 'and what a small world it is, I find I live about ten minutes' drive from Curtis's place! Isn't it strange? Uncle Kevin's mentioned his name to me often over the years, but I've never actually met him before. Have you known him long, Charlotte?'

Chatting. The chatter had never ceased from the moment Charlie had arrived. The party was in fact going with a swing, conversation flitting back and forth across the vast mahogany dining-table, becoming a little more animated as wine glasses were refilled and then refilled again.

Charlotte had had only the briefest private exchange with Curtis, soon after she'd been delivered by the chauffeur. 'Ah, it's the lady in white,' he'd said with a smile. 'You look lovely, Charlotte. And how was the wedding?'

'Perfect.' One word, that's all she'd said when really she wanted to demand of him what he wanted of her, exactly, what he thought he'd been doing in fixing this invitation. She hadn't wanted to come! And now that she had, what did she find? Pippa, beautiful and far more sophisticated, making a play for Curtis quite openly!

Charlotte had been taken over by Sir Kevin at that point, invited to see the paintings in Loxley Hall. Even as she had left the room with her host, Pippa had slid her arm under Curtis's, had been looking up at him smilingly.

The man on Charlie's left touched her arm, his grin a little unpleasant as he spoke. 'Looks as though old Pippa's found her next victim,' he muttered.

Her face impassive, Charlie looked at him and made no comment. What was this, sour grapes? The man was in his early forties, had arrived alone just after Charlotte had got there. All she knew about him was that much and that his name was Dean. And that he'd had one glass too many already. She followed his glare, found Pippa on the receiving end of it, not that she noticed. She was deep in conversation with Curtis.

'She's a past master,' Dean went on, 'at casting the line and catching. Always lands 'em.'

Feeling obliged to say something, Charlie smiled. 'She's a very beautiful woman. And you,' she added pleasantly, 'clearly agree with me. You can't take your eyes off her.'

'I've been in love with her for the past fifteen years.' The announcement was made flatly, hopelessly. 'If I'd known she was going to be up here this weekend, I wouldn't have accepted Kevin's invitation.'

Snap, thought Charlie. Sir Kevin spoke to her at that point. He had been charming to her throughout the evening, yet she wondered why he'd bothered inviting her. 'Charlotte, my niece seems to be monopolising Curtis. You're not going to stand by and allow it, are you? He was so keen for you to come here tonight—as I was, of course—but you two hardly seem to have spoken to one another.' He was clearly intrigued, if not at a loss.

She had to think, fast, for a suitable response. 'I don't know what Curtis has told you, Sir Kevin, but he and I hardly know one another, really. I can't say I blame him for being interested in your niece, she's very lovely.'

Sir Kevin blinked at that. He started to nod in agreement, then he looked at Charlotte with open curiosity, as if she'd said the last thing he had expected her to say.

But in fact Curtis was not interested in Pippa Loxley. Charlotte realised that. In spite of herself she had been keeping an eye on him, without appearing to, of course. Time and again she had felt his eyes on her while she'd been talking to the men on either side of her. Time and again their eyes had inevitably met and she had been quick to look away, to avoid the question in them. He was far too sensitive to atmosphere not to realise she was angry with him.

No, he wasn't interested in Pippa. Right now she was openly flirting with him, but it wasn't having the desired effect. He was looking at Charlotte again, she could feel it even as she kept her attention fully on Sir Kevin and what he was saying. Her host was talking about food now, about his likes and dislikes.

Pippa, she thought as she listened, you're playing it all wrong. You're making it too easy for him. He'll find it no fun at all if you make yourself so obvious.

And there was Charlotte's answer. Wasn't it equally obvious what Curtis wanted of her? He had as much as told her he liked the fun of the chase. What a nerve he had! Well, Charlie was one challenge he would discover he just wasn't up to. He hadn't a hope of getting her into bed, not a hope! It was impossible for her to behave as though she didn't know who Chris was, impossible, not that she was the type in any case to go jumping into bed with a man just because she was attracted to him. She was far from that.

As these thoughts were going through her mind, she glanced over at him, her eyes telling plainly of her indignation.

Later, when the party was gathered in the drawing-room after dinner, Curtis made a point of coming over to Charlotte, interrupting the conversation she was having with a married couple.

'Excuse me.' He looked at the other two, not at Charlie. Placing a hand very firmly under her elbow, he added, 'I'd like a word with Charlotte alone.'

Once out of the earshot of others, he demanded, 'What the hell's the matter with you? Kevin's just told me you're about to go home.'

'It's almost midnight,' she said reasonably. 'And I shan't be the first to leave.' She had seen to that, had waited a respectable length of time before saying she must be on her way.

'That's not what I'm talking about. Why did you ask for the chauffeur to take you home?'

'He brought me, didn't he?'

Curtis's eyes flashed at her angrily. 'That couldn't be helped. In the circumstances it wasn't appropriate that I should fetch you. Besides, Kevin and I were talking business until people started arriving.'

Wanting only to get away, to keep things pleasant for Sir Kevin's sake, Charlotte smiled with all the grace she could muster. 'I don't see what the fuss is about, Curtis. It makes no difference to me who takes me home.'

'It makes a lot of difference to me. I want to talk to

you, and this is hardly the place for it. Say your goodbyes and I'll bring my car round to the front.'

'I don't want to go home with——'

The pressure of his fingers bit into her arm, stopping her as she gasped. 'This has been a very strange evening as it is,' he said under his breath. 'Thanks to you. I've had enough of your nonsense, Charlotte. You can stop looking daggers at me as of *now*. One more word of protest from you and I shall pick you up and throw you into my car! *I* am taking you home.'

She looked at him, her eyes bright with challenge. Should she? Dare she? He was such an unknown quantity. Was he as furious as he appeared to be? He wouldn't really do as he'd threatened, would he? No, of course he wouldn't! She looked up at him, laughing. 'Thanks all the same, but the chauffeur will be waiting for me now.'

As she turned away from him she felt his arms go around her waist, heard the exasperation in his voice as he said, 'O.K., you asked for it.'

'No!' She almost shouted the word. Dear Lord, he'd meant it! Rapidly her arms closed over his and she stiffened, lowering her voice at once. 'All right, all right! I'll go—I mean I'll come. Let go of me, for heaven's sake! Everyone's looking!'

Then minutes later they were driving in silence.

It was a clear night, moonlit, starlit, warm. Charlotte pressed the button which would open her window, leaving it half-way down, volunteering no conversation at all.

Unpredictable though he undoubtedly was, she wasn't surprised when Curtis pulled off the road and parked in a deserted country lane. He switched off the engine and turned to her. 'All right, Charlotte, supposing you tell me what I've done to annoy you? I've tried working it out, tried and failed. So what's up now?'

She could handle him now. Her dislike of him had returned and had increased so that she was able at last to handle him as she'd intended to handle him last Tuesday. 'Curtis, I think we're both sufficiently adult that we can cut out the games.'

'Games?' He simply looked at her. 'If you're talking about Pippa's performance, let me assure you——'

'You don't need to assure me. You're not in the least interested in Pippa. You had the misfortune to find yourself seated next to her. I've no doubt she wangled that. You didn't appreciate her flirting. It's me you're after.'

She had the satisfaction of seeing his eyebrows go up. She shrugged. 'You're an attractive man, I'm duly flattered. But you're wasting your time.' Coolly but pleasantly she added, 'I'm not interested, Curtis. I've told you. It seems that it's you who needs to be told everything twice. If you'll . . .' As she went on he started smiling, the most audacious smile she'd seen in her life. He knew she was lying, knew damn well she was lying! It almost stopped her. But not quite. 'If you'll stop and think about it, I haven't spent any time in your company willingly. You've used your influence and power to get me to spend time with you. Including this dinner tonight. I didn't want to go. Believe me, I went to please my parents. Sir Kevin is not someone my father would want to offend in any way.'

There was silence. After a moment, as if snapping himself out of a fascinating reverie he said, exaggeratedly, 'Oh! Have you finished? Is that the end of your lovely little tirade?'

Charlotte's mouth straightened into a tight line. God, he was irritating. He was *still* laughing at her! What did she have to do to convince him? 'Yes.'

'Then supposing you tell me what's really bugging you? Since we're supposed not to be playing games.'

He was right. She had cornered herself nicely,

hadn't she? She looked him straight in the eye. 'Then supposing you tell me who Chris is?'

'Chris?' His expression changed. A frown replaced the smile. For a moment he seemed disconcerted, as if wondering how Charlotte knew about Chris. Then he remembered the phone call. With a hint of residual puzzlement he said, 'Chris is my sister. Why?'

Charlotte's face, fully visible to him in the moonlight, said it all. His smile came back. 'I see,' he said slowly. 'You assumed Christine—Chris—was a girl-friend, right?'

Oh, God! Charlie almost groaned aloud. Rarely had she felt so stupid. His *sister*! No, she hadn't assumed anything. She had been informed, misinformed, that ... Her mother's words came back to her loud and clear ... 'You could have the wrong end of the stick.'

Margaret! Oh, *Maggie*! Do you know by now? Do you know who Chris is? You might have told me!

But why should she? What did she expect, for Margaret to say, 'Oh, by the way, I had it all wrong about Chris. It turns out she's his sister.' Margaret wouldn't have found much fun in that!

In the face of her silence, Curtis shrugged. 'Maybe I should have mentioned it when I phoned her yesterday, but I thought nothing of it. No wonder you were acting strangely when I left.'

'Can we go, please? I'm awfully tired.' She was awfully embarrassed if he did but know it!

He knew it. 'In a minute. You've misjudged me, you will now hear me out.' He went on quietly, unemotionally, a man making a statement of fact. 'There have been a lot of women in my life, Charlotte— I adore them, I've told you that. But there are never two at the same time, not in the sense we're talking about. Not as lovers. Never, ever. On principle. Remember that.'

She looked at him, their eyes meeting and holding for seconds before he turned away and started the engine. They weren't far from her parents' house, just a few minutes, but in those few minutes she found her mind racing with a jumble of thoughts and emotions.

He had told her the truth, not for one second did she doubt Chris was his sister. *Why* was she so relieved? Why, suddenly, did she wish she had behaved more rationally with him all along, why was she wishing now that this evening didn't have to end so soon? Why, why, was she feeling so foolishly happy?

Not that it showed. She was quiet for the rest of the journey, grateful as Curtis made a few comments about the dinner party, about Sir Kevin and his guests. She knew precisely what he was doing, he was easing things back on to a normal footing, aware that he'd given her food for thought. He could, she realised, be very tactful when he wanted to be. And charming. And sensitive.

And stubborn and forceful and sarcastic.

Yes, but he also had a good sense of humour. She'd always liked that about him, regardless of anything else.

He didn't switch off the engine as he pulled up, but he got out of the car, saying he would see her to the door. The house was in darkness except for the hall light. Her parents, of course, were in bed. It was almost one o'clock. Had she been standing outside her own flat, Charlotte would have invited him in for a cup of coffee. But she wasn't at her own home, and Curtis clearly didn't expect to be asked in.

'Well, good night, Curtis.' She gave him a smile which was, she hoped, one of straightforward friendship.

He responded likewise. There was nothing deliberately seductive about him, yet she found her eyes moving fleetingly to his mouth. She checked herself, made a point of looking in her bag for the door key. When his hand closed over hers as she extracted the key, she almost jumped. It made no sense to her, no sense at all, but she wished he would kiss her. Only yesterday she had almost dreaded his doing so, but now . . . She let go, let him take the key and turn it in the lock.

'Safely delivered,' he murmured. Then, moving away from her slightly, 'I thought we'd got over our bad start. Perhaps we should begin all over again now we've sorted a few things out. Starting tomorrow, what do you say?'

She nodded, hoping her wish didn't show in her eyes, hoping her expression was friendly and nothing else. 'Agreed.'

He seemed satisfied. 'I'll pick you up at ten. O.K. with you?'

'Since when do you ask?' she said impishly. 'You dictate, I obey.'

'That's just how it should be!' He was half-way down the drive, laughing now. 'Good night, Charlotte.'

'Night-night.'

For a long time, she looked at herself in the mirror on her dressing table. 'Night-night?' She hadn't used that phrase since she was little! Why was she feeling so light-hearted? Light-hearted and . . . unsatisfied. He hadn't given her as much as a good night peck—even on the nose! But yesterday, in the car, if she'd given him the slightest encouragement he would have . . . Even the thought of it had her heart pounding. If being held in his arms was half as good as the anticipation of it, it would be . . . Tomorrow she must tell her mother about Chris. Give her the satisfaction of saying I told you so. Charlotte would laugh when she did, would allow her mum to gloat a bit. That didn't matter, what mattered was that her mother didn't think badly of Curtis.

The drive home to London on Sunday was fun. They talked incessantly, stopping for coffee and again for a leisurely lunch and talking, talking, getting to know one another's points of view, likes and dislikes. They found one another interesting, amusing, it was as simple as that, and the hours of the long journey sped by frustratingly fast.

They got to Charlie's flat around seven; she didn't hesitate to ask him in for a cuppa, and Curtis didn't hesitate to accept. An hour later he was cooking omelettes in her small but well-equipped kitchen.

'Hey, I'm impressed!' She sat, watching him, her face in her hands, her elbows on her knees.

'My dear Charlotte,' he said loftily, 'not only am I far nicer than you thought I was, I'm also quite talented. Well, in the kitchen at least! Well—at making omelettes, anyway!'

She giggled. 'You didn't learn to make omelettes at Charterhouse!'

Charterhouse. That's where he'd been educated. And later at Cambridge. He'd told her a little about his childhood, about his parents. His father had been the one to provoke in him a feeling for, an interest in, art. A private collector himself, as was his father before him, Montgomery Maxwell had taught his son all he knew. It had been during his university years that Curtis had decided to make art his life, his career.

'But your father had no hand in your business?' she'd asked.

'My father was a barrister. He died, both my parents died, while I was at Cambridge. He had a hand in the opening of my first gallery in so far as it was his money that funded it. My family's wealthy,' he'd added matter-of-factly. 'Not only did my father make a lot, he inherited a lot. It was passed on to me and Chris, naturally.'

'And you've made more money. Seven galleries, Curtis! You've done a lot in a short time.'

He'd laughed at that. 'A short time? You know how old I am, I've been at it for years. Why, it was you who pointed out I'm at a grand old age, was it not?'

And the conversation had reverted to her at that point. Now, watching him as he poured beaten eggs into an omelette pan, she asked, 'Is Chris married?'

'No.'

Charlie wished she could see his face, but he had his back to her just then. There had been ... something not quite right in the way he'd said the single syllable.

'Where does she live?' She asked this because like the previous one it was a natural question, even though she knew the answer.

'In the Cotswolds, not far from Cheltenham.'

'Does she——'

'Hey!' Curtis interrupted her, turned to look at her with a grin. 'Don't just sit there, you bone-idle chatterbox, set the table. This'll be ready in a minute.'

'Yes, sir. Yes, sir.' Charlotte busied herself at once. 'Of course, if you were *really* an efficient cook, you'd manage to do it all yourself. I mean, you've told me, in that modest way of yours, how *nice* and how *clever* you are, what would you do if you were giving a dinner party?'

'Don't ask silly questions, Charlotte, I'd bring caterers in! What else?'

The flat seemed abnormally quiet after he left. He went at ten, quite suddenly announcing his departure. His departure, though not his attitude, seemed abrupt. Considering they were listening to a record she had put on at his request ...

'It's time I went.' She looked up, surprised by the words, to find his eyes on her.

'Oh! I——' She didn't want to show her disappointment but in spite of herself she asked whether something were wrong.

Already on his feet, Curtis looked down at her, thinking before he answered. 'There's ... no, nothing's wrong. No, don't get up. I can see myself out.'

Not only was she a little mystified, she was also

feeling very unsure of herself. She stayed where she was, sitting on the floor, her long legs stretched out, her back against the settee which faced the armchair he'd occupied. Why this abrupt departure? Had he had too much of her company today? They'd been together all day and all evening. Had she begun to bore him? It was such an unwelcome notion that she found herself asking him, albeit in a jocular way, 'Bored, eh? Record or no record, enough is enough!'

The smile began at his mouth, slowly, spread to his eyes and stayed there as he shook his head. 'You don't believe that for one minute.' With slow deliberation his eyes moved over her, inch by inch, from head to foot and back again. 'It's been a lovely day, Charlotte. Thank you. And—good night.'

She stood by the window, listening as the engine of the Jaguar fired into action in the courtyard below. It was tempting to pull back the curtain and look down, but she wouldn't do it. Instead she closed her eyes, moved away from the light against the window and stood with her back against the wall of her living-room. A moment later she switched off the stereo and listened instead to the abnormal silence of the room. She had never heard this before. She wished he hadn't gone.

Dear God in heaven, she thought with a start. I'm missing him already!

In the courtyard, from the car, Curtis looked up at the window of Charlotte's flat, a smile of satisfaction on his lips. We'll see what we shall see, my lovely, he thought.

Ah, but it had not been easy to leave her, not at all easy! The smile vanished. He kept his eyes on the window, wondering about her. As he did so a frown pulled his brows together. Fascinating, she was altogether too damned fascinating. It wasn't normally like this. There was something wrong somewhere. What was it? What was wrong? He hadn't been away from her five minutes and he was already planning on when he'd speak to her tomorrow . . .

Charlotte went into her bedroom, her movements slow, automatic. She unzipped her suitcase and pulled out the contents, sorting washing and dry-cleaning. Good night and thank you, he'd said. He hadn't even wanted to kiss her, let alone attempted to. And he'd said not a word about getting in touch, not a word about—well, about anything that mattered.

CHAPTER SIX

THE call came at nine the following morning. Charlotte had been in the office for precisely one minute. Her secretary had arrived before her.

She picked up the phone, pulling a face at Linda as she did so. 'Someone's bright and early,' she muttered.

'What was that about bright and early?'

'Curtis!' The word was an explosion of pleasure. Charlie could have kicked herself; Linda was looking on, obviously amused. 'I was just saying that someone's bright and early!'

'Hardly. I've been in my office for over an hour.' His tone was businesslike, disappointingly so. It deceived her into thinking this wasn't a personal call. She was wrong.

'I've been checking my diary,' he went on. 'Couldn't commit myself to anything until I did. I suppose there's no point in asking you to have supper after you finish these rehearsals of yours?'

'No point at all,' she agreed, though her pulses were pounding, making her suddenly light-headed. She had spent so much time wondering and worrying last night, convinced she wasn't going to hear from him again. 'It's just that I'm—I have to be practical, Curtis. The rehearsals are a strain, specially since we're getting closer to the performance, and I have things to do when I get in, have to be up for work—— '

'It's O.K.' There was a smile in his voice. 'You know I'm not the pushy type.'

Charlie was smiling, too, aware of Linda's interest since she made no pretence not to be listening. Not the pushy type? Not much!

'Well, at least we can lunch together,' Curtis was saying. 'I have business lunches today and Friday but I can see you tomorrow, Wednesday and Thursday. You name the time. I mean, I wouldn't want to appear to be dictating to you, Charlotte . . .'

'Far be it from you . . .' she mocked. It didn't occur to her, simply did not occur to her to say no.

Nor did it occur to her to stop and think about what had happened in the space of a week, just one week. She looked forward to Tuesday's lunch with an eagerness which was alien to her. Oh, she had looked forward to things in the past, to holidays, parties and so on. But this? She couldn't wait to see Curtis again.

It was difficult, trying to remain friendly but casual during those times together that week. But she couldn't, wouldn't, let him see how keen she was, how interested. Curtis, on the other hand, showed no such restraint. He was charming, amusing, entertaining, allowing his own interest full rein. He was also demonstrative—sort of. Whether they were walking to or from Charlie's office or whether they were going by taxi, it was always hand in hand. Always, he reached for her hand as he met her on the steps of the gallery, as they left the restaurant. They went to three different places on those three consecutive days, places with atmosphere and good food, places where Curtis was greeted by name and shown to the best table.

That, however, was as far as it went. She was at a loss to understand it, that he made no attempt to do more than hold her hand. It was by no means unheard-of for people to be seen kissing in the back of a London taxi. Curtis made no attempt to do so, didn't give her so much as a perfunctory peck. She told herself that it wasn't his style to take a woman in his arms in public, albeit while in a cab. Nevertheless it bothered her. It bothered her very much, to the extent that she was beginning to wonder whether she'd been misreading him all along. No, that wasn't possible.

The attraction was there between them, undeniably, getting stronger every time they met. She could almost reach out and touch it, that's how strong it was; and they both felt it, she was sure of that. So why did he make no attempt to take her in his arms? Why was her longing for it becoming an obsession? By the time Thursday rolled around, when he was dropping her off at work, it was all she could do not to demand to be kissed!

Charlie had had a lot of teasing and questioning to cope with, teasing from Linda and questions from Geoffrey Hemmings.

'What's happened to you?' This, from Geoffrey, the minute he'd called at her flat on the Monday night to take her to rehearsal. She had affected not to know what he was talking about but, when he asked her what had happened since he'd last seen her, asked about her weekend, she told him. Why shouldn't she? At least, she told him as much as she cared for him to know.

She reacted similarly with Linda, telling her only what she wanted her to know. In her secretary's case, perforce it had to be even less than she told Geoffrey. Linda, however, was Charlie's full-time companion, contemporary, and she was female to boot. She knew long before Charlie what had happened to her—but she had the wisdom to say nothing, to stop the teasing as soon as she realised.

There was no problem at all with Mr Grant. As far as Charlie knew, the big boss had no idea about the lunches she was having with Curtis. Even so, he wouldn't have pried, not only because it was not in his nature but also because he continued to be distracted with his own affairs.

'Curtis?' She spoke quietly as the taxi drew to a halt near the steps to the College Gallery on Thursday. 'You haven't said much since we left the restaurant, is something wrong?'

She was becoming insecure, beginning to doubt her

own power of attraction even though she knew how much he was attracted to her. Her hand was in his, held firmly by long, strong fingers.

'Of course not. I—was just thinking about the weekend. I mean this weekend.'

'What about it?' Her eyes were smiling at him, she was waiting, expecting him to suggest they had dinner. She was free, he knew that, knew she didn't rehearse at the weekend.

'I'm going to the Cotswolds tomorrow evening. Going to see Chris.'

'Oh.' Charlotte couldn't help it—the sound told of her disappointment. He was going to see his sister.

'I often do.' Was there something defensive about this? 'I like to spend time with her when I can, when I'm free.'

'Of course.' She kept her smile in place but her disappointment was acute. When he was free? But what about her, Charlotte? Surely he wouldn't rather be with his sister than—

Evidently, he would.

'I think that's nice,' she said brightly. 'Keeping in touch like that. If I had a brother or sister I'd——'

'Charlotte, I——'

She broke off at once, listening, watching. But he said no more. Even when she prompted him, he never finished what he'd been going to say. 'Go on. What were you going to tell me?'

'Nothing. Just that I'll ring you next week—early next week, all right?'

'Very much so.' When he leaned forward to open the taxi door, she stepped out, making a continued effort to hide her disappointment, to keep the bright smile on her face.

Well, she had her own plans for the weekend . . . but her evenings would be free.

She spent the day shopping on Saturday. She wanted a skirt length of black cloth, something cheap and easy to sew. Gloria Ackroyd needed an outfit, and Charlie had it very clearly pictured in her mind. The top which would go with the skirt had already been bought, she'd found it in C & A a couple of weeks earlier, a stretchy, rib-hugging thing in a ghastly shade of purple. The top and the skirt she would make during the weekend were just the thing for the character she was portraying in the play. Oh, yes, she wanted some perfume, too. A bottle of cheap and nasty.

Something had to be done with Saturday evening. There was nothing on the telly. It would be all too easy to ring upstairs, to ask Geoffrey to come down and put in a bit more rehearsal. But her heart wouldn't be in it. Besides, since it was Saturday he was probably out. Nor would it be fair to use Geoffrey like that; she didn't want to rehearse, she wanted company—*Curtis's* company.

So Charlotte put on a record, drifted into her bedroom and did some experimenting with Gloria's make-up instead. She was glad she had. She couldn't get it right. She was putting on either too little or too much, ending up with the look of an archetypal prostitute, an absence of authenticity.

By Sunday lunchtime she had finished the skirt, machine-hemmed as it was. She wriggled herself into it and laughed aloud at the hip-hugging tightness of it. That, together with the purple stretch top, certainly put her in the mood of the character! She kept the skirt and top on, satisfied with them, and started on her face again. Maybe she would get the make-up just right now, since she was wearing Gloria's clothes. The perfume! Perhaps if she put some on, if she told herself it was nice rather than offensive, she would really connect with the character. That had been her idea when buying it.

It worked. It worked even better when she thought Gloria's thoughts, forgetting her own psyche as she went over her lines, putting on make-up, talking to herself in the dressing-table mirror.

It was around two o'clock when the doorbell rang, startling her. Pleased with herself, Charlotte walked quickly to answer it. It would be Geoffrey, she didn't doubt. She was eager to know what he thought of the make-up, the outfit . . .

But it wasn't Geoffrey. It was Curtis. He was smiling as Charlie opened the door, leaning against the frame and saying, 'I just happened to be—*good God!*' He gaped at her, unable to believe what he was seeing. 'Charlotte! What *is* this? Are you indulging in some kinky fantasy or do you have a secret life?'

Once over the shock of seeing him, she'd started laughing. She was prostrate now, helpless at the look on his face.

'Answer me, woman!' His lips were twitching, his horror turning to mere perplexity. 'What have you got round your *eyes* for heaven's sake? And what the devil is that smell you're wearing?' He was laughing with her now. At her. With her. At himself. 'I mean, what—what's going *on*? Charlotte, you look for all the world like the cheapest kind of street-walker!'

Delighted, she doubled up; no way could she stop laughing. With her right hand she held on to her stomach, with her left, she beckoned him in. He was still on the landing, the door wide open, his deep voice booming unchecked.

'I'm not sure I want to come in,' he said, coming in. He closed the door and gave vent fully to his own laughter. 'Don't tell me, all you've shown me so far is your persona, the face you present to the world, yes? But you're really Charlotte the harlot, right?'

'Right!' She had never laughed so much, she laughed until her stomach ached, hardly able to stutter through an explanation. 'The play. It's—I'm—for the play, you idiot!'

'That's your story.' Curtis sank into an armchair,

hooked an ankle over a knee and continued to survey her. 'If you laugh this much when you're entertaining your clients, you'll never get rich, dearie. If there's one thing a man dislikes its being laughed at when——'

'Stop it! Oh, stop, please!' He was winding her up even more, sending her into fits. She sobered only when she started hiccupping. 'What are you doing here, Curtis? I thought you——'

He held up a hand, his head moving from side to side. 'I can't stand it. That black stuff around your eyes—you look awful. Ill. Take it off! And for heaven's sake, and mine, wash the rest of you while you're about it!'

She spread her hands, grinning now. 'I'm playing a prostitute, an ageing, pathetic creature whose life has reached crisis point, breaking point.'

'If you don't stop looking at me through that mask, I think I'm going to have some kind of breakdown myself.' Curtis's eyes roamed over her as she stood in the middle of the living-room floor. Red patent (plastic) four-inch stilettos. Black stockings, laddered in one leg. Skirt with a split in one side, about eight inches. Purple boob-tube, leaving little to the imagination.

He groaned. 'Off with it! All of it. Starting with the face!'

Charlotte looked hurt. Hamming it up, she pouted sulkily. 'You don't like my outfit, Curtis?'

His eyes flitted to the top of the split in the skirt, noting the hint of stocking top. 'The skirt's a dream,' he grinned. 'I could even get used to that purple paint on your torso—but the make-up, I could never live with that!'

Laughing again, Charlotte retreated and went into her bedroom. She slapped a handful of cream on her face and removed it with tissues as best she could. Then, because it was by far the quickest thing to do, she stripped off and stepped under the shower, soaping herself quickly and thoroughly. Back in her bedroom she glanced fleetingly at her full-length dressing-gown and decided against it, pulling on jeans and a tee-shirt instead.

She found Curtis in the kitchen, making coffee. He turned as she approached, smiling at him, fresh-faced now and smelling only of soap. There was a new ripple of laughter from both of them, but it was quickly gone. They stood, two feet apart, looking at each other.

'Hello,' he said softly.

'Hello, Curtis.'

'It's good to see you.' It was a whisper.

'It's good to see you, too.'

They moved at exactly the same time, Charlotte's arms sliding around his neck, his arms circling her waist. He held her, still making no attempt to kiss her, his eyes smiling down into hers. Exasperated, she lifted her face. 'Kiss me!' she demanded. 'Curtis Maxwell, if you don't kiss me this very instant, I shall have a nervous breakdown!'

'Why, Miss Graham,' he laughed, a sound of satisfaction, 'I thought you'd never ask!'

They kissed with all the hunger and longing of people who had been denied for too long. Again and again they kissed, clinging together as they stood, discovering, tasting, exploring.

'Oh, Charlotte!' His hands moved to the back of her head, holding her face against his neck as her arms moved around his back, holding him closer, closer.

For a moment she stood, face buried against his neck, acknowledging what his body was telling her, bewildered by the intensity of her own response. His arousal had been so swift, so fervent . . .

She stepped away from him, only her eyes keeping contact now, compelled as they were to his. Her small, perfectly shaped breasts were rising and falling beneath the thin skin of her tee-shirt. 'Have you—have you had lunch?' She turned away from him, busying herself by adding milk to the coffee.

'No.' There was amusement in his voice. 'And you?'

'No. I was too busy with Gloria, remember?' She faced him then, her gold-flecked hazel eyes lit up with laughter.

'So when's the actual performance? Or should I say performances?'

'This Wednesday is the first night. It runs till Saturday.'

'I'll be there,' he told her. 'On the first night. Can't wait—I love a night out at the theatre.'

The theatre! She was laughing again. 'No, Curtis. I hardly think this is your scene. The audience will be made up mainly of senior citizens who couldn't afford a night at a real theatre even if they wanted one. The church hall gets stuffy in this weather and the chairs are of the Sunday school variety.'

'Am I to take it you don't want me there?'

She really wasn't sure. 'I—think I'd be embarrassed.'

'That's ridiculous!'

'Maybe.' She shrugged. 'About lunch—I'm starving! Shall we have this coffee and then go out for something to eat?'

Curtis stood, watching her, arms folded as he leaned against the fridge-freezer. 'If that's what you'd like to do. All right, I know a nice little pub down by the river, where we can eat outside.'

It was a glorious afternoon, weather-wise and in every other respect. Hand in hand, they walked along the banks of the Thames after lunch, in silence for once, just enjoying each other.

'You—came back from the Cotswolds early,' she said at length, bending to pick up a buttercup.

Curtis took the flower and held it under her chin, his vivid blue eyes smiling into hers. 'I missed you,' he said simply.

When they separated at seven o'clock, it was only for an hour. Curtis dropped her outside her building and said he would be back for her at eight. He was going home to change. They were going somewhere 'splendid' for dinner. She must dress up, she'd been told. They kissed before they parted, but it was different this time. There was no haste, no particular hunger, just a long, slow, heartfelt kiss which left them both, none the less, yearning for more. Much more.

What should she wear? She rummaged through her wardrobe and selected a dress of the colour redheads weren't supposed to wear. Red. Holding it against her, she looked in the full-length mirror. No, it was too dramatic, not right for tonight. It was too hot for red. She wanted to look, to feel, cool. Even if it were only an illusion. A simple but elegant dress of palest yellow proved the solution. Sleeveless, cut into a plunging V, traced around the neckline with gold thread. Medium-heeled sandals in exactly the same shade.

Hair up or down? Down. Curtis liked it just as it was, loose, doing its own thing but never in an untidy way. Perfume? St. Laurent's Opium, what else? Rather different from what she'd been wearing earlier!

As Charlotte dressed in the silence of her bedroom, she thought very carefully about the hours ahead. When Curtis had asked her what she would like to do with the evening, she had wanted to say, 'Let's go to your flat, I want to see your paintings.'

She laughed aloud. What a line that would have been! She could just imagine Curtis's reaction to that! Something like, 'Well, I've heard some pretty good seduction lines in my time, but that isn't one of them.'

Except, of course, that she meant it. As he would have realised only too well. But . . .

But she didn't want to invite herself into his home, into his bachelor pad. She didn't want . . .

She closed her eyes. Of course she wanted! Wanted him. She'd wanted him right from the start. She had, she realised as she put the finishing touches to her make-up, a decision to make. Tonight.

'Alas, there's no dancing here on Sundays.' Hours later, as they lingered over coffee and brandy, Curtis reached across the table for her hand.

They had driven south of the river to a restaurant she hadn't been to before. It was small enough to be intimate, big enough to have a dance floor, the postage-stamp type. Beyond it was a shallow platform where the musicians would play. It was just as well, she thought, because if they had been dancing in these surroundings, after a superb dinner, such a wonderful day . . .

His fingers were caressing her hand, stroking, circling, sending sparks of excitement to every other part of her body. Almost unwillingly her eyes moved to his. Suddenly there were no conversations, no one else in the room.

'Are you ready to go home, Charlotte?'

Her voice was barely more than a whisper. 'Yes.' But she swallowed as she said it. Uncertain, still uncertain.

She was in his arms even before they got into his car, standing in the blackness of the night, in the silence of the car park.

'Charlotte——' Curtis's voice was low, urgent against her lips. 'I want you, God, how I want you!'

They drove to her flat in silence, a silence which spoke volumes. He knew, he knew exactly what she was thinking, how nervous she was, how she was feeling. Didn't he always? He knew of her ambivalence, she was certain of that.

When they reached her front door, he took her key from her hand and pushed it into the lock. But he made no move to go in. Very quietly, with two fingers tilting her face up, he asked, 'Well, Charlotte? Are you inviting me in?'

She closed her eyes, didn't want to look at him as she answered. 'No, I—don't think so, Curtis.'

For a moment he didn't move, didn't speak. With a pounding heart she waited, knowing she would be lost if he kissed her, knowing how very easily he could change her mind for her.

But Curtis didn't do that. His fingers moved to her hair, sliding briefly into the tumble of loose curls. 'So be it.'

Her eyes came open, questioning, worrying. 'When will I see you?'

'On Wednesday. I told you.'

She watched as he walked away, turned the corner which led to the stairs. Out of sight. Never out of mind.

It was only as she got into bed that she remembered: the first night of the play was a sell-out, there were no more tickets available for Wednesday.

CHAPTER SEVEN

THE applause went on and on. And on!

Charlotte, still high on adrenalin, took a bow on her own, gratified at the sudden increase in the applause. Her eyes scanned the audience, but she could see no further than the first few rows, the church hall was too dark beyond that. Curtis wasn't here, he couldn't be. She hadn't really supposed he'd been serious about coming.

It had been three days since she'd seen him. The longest days of her life. The only hours when he hadn't been in her mind had been when she was rehearsing. Even during the break in last night's dress rehearsal, she'd thought about him, had wondered what he was doing, where he was. There had been no phone call but, this morning, there had been a card in the post at home. It had said simply, 'Thinking about you. Good luck for tonight. Curtis.'

The curtain fell, congratulations were bandied about among the stage crew and the smiling cast of *Count Your Regrets at Midnight*. There was a hubbub of chatter backstage and, shortly afterwards, in the dressing-rooms.

'It went well, didn't it?'

'The play went down well, I wouldn't say we did well. Geoffrey and I, I mean.'

'You mean the hiccup in Act Two. I heard it, I was cringing for you!'

There were two dressing-rooms, one for males and one for females. Charlie was removing her make-up, talking ten to the dozen with one of the other women when Sandra Evans, the girl who had prompted, came in with a bouquet of flowers.

'I say!' Sandra, tall, skinny and very plum-in-the-mouth, handed the bouquet to Charlie with a flourish. 'Who *is* he, Charlie? Talk about tall, blond and handsome!'

There was no answer. Charlotte was staring at the twelve red roses under Cellophane. There was no card with them, but there was no mistaking who they were from, not after Sandra's remark. Either there had been some cancellations or else Curtis must have turned on the charm to get a seat.

'Well, don't just sit there, finish what you're doing and get changed. The man is waiting for you!'

'So he is here!' Charlie said unnecessarily.

'There's no doubt about that, dear! He's out there with some of the oldies who're waiting to shake your hand. You and your leading man.'

Giggling at Sandra's choice of words, she hastily removed the rest of the make-up and changed her clothes.

Geoffrey was peeved when she tried to extract herself a little later. There was a group of people in the church hall, the cast and some of the audience. Curtis towered over them by inches, holding Charlotte's arm under his and smiling at the 'Well done!' and the congratulations she was getting.

She could understand Geoffrey's feelings. Oh, he had had his fair share of congratulations, of praise, but it was by tacit understanding that the cast went across the road for a drink together after the first night. They always did.

Charlie wanted to get away, to go with Curtis for the supper he had suggested. She wasn't going to refuse tonight! If she were late for work tomorrow, too bad. Yet she felt awkward, as if she were being disloyal to her friends. 'Would you mind?' she murmured to Curtis. 'We could just pop across the road and have one drink with them. On the first night, we always——'

'I understand. I don't mind.'

'Do you mean it?'

'No!' He smiled at her, hugging her arm more tightly beneath his. 'But I'll do it. Come on.'

'It'll do you good,' she teased, 'to see how the other half lives.' She was thinking about the Jolly Roger pub across the road, it wasn't quite the sort of place Curtis normally drank in, that was for sure.

By contrast, the place where they ate supper was luxurious, though in fact it was nowhere special. Just a Greek taverna not too far from Charlie's home. Dressed in the clothes she'd worn to work that day and with a face devoid of make-up, she had told Curtis not to take her anywhere swish.

So they settled for kebabs with aubergines and rice and it was ... passable. Washed down with a fairly decent red wine it was O.K.

'This is hardly the celebration I had in mind,' Curtis told her. 'I wanted to take you——'

'It doesn't matter.' Charlotte was too high to care about what she was eating or where she was. Curtis was here, the play had gone down astonishingly well. 'I made a mess of it, you know. Act Two, at the beginning of the scene. I fed Geoffrey quite the wrong line, poor thing. Did you notice?'

'I can't say I did. He obviously coped, it all flowed on logically.'

'One has to cope. Then he did it to me in the third act, jumped from one speech to another. I stalled for time, put in a few movements which weren't supposed to be there. Do you remember, when I crossed the stage and got the cigarettes? I wasn't supposed to do that just then. Still, I covered the clanger. Must have, if it all looked and sounded all right. That's amateur dramatics for you. Still, I'm sure things like that must happen on the professional stage.'

'I'm sure they do.' Curtis was smiling at her enthusiasm, enjoying it, enjoying her and the way she looked. Her face looked lovely, freshly washed and without a trace of make-up, her freckles ... Her freckles! His mind drifted for a moment. He was back in the car with her, recalling the day they'd driven home from the Lake District, laughing at her indignation when he'd called her Freckles. 'Don't!' she'd protested. 'I hate them! Hate them! When I was little I put sour cream on them, and lemon juice. I was told it would make them fade away or something. Old wives' tales! Nothing can get rid of them, I'm stuck with them for ever.' And all his reassurances seemed to have no effect. He, personally, adored those freckles.

'Curtis!' she was saying now. 'I've lost you. I'm rambling, I know. Sorry!'

He caught hold of her left hand, covered it with both of his. 'Don't be. Charlotte Amanda Graham, you are a delight. Never, never apologise for being yourself. I love seeing you like this. And, though I'm ready for your protest, let me tell you how very beautiful you're looking right now.'

That quietened her. Beautiful—he'd never called her that before. Attractive, very attractive, yes. But never beautiful. Though he appeared absolutely sincere, she laughed it off and started chattering again. It was just as well she had come out for a couple of hours. She wouldn't have slept if she'd gone straight home, she never could after a first night, she was always too keyed up.

In the car on the way back to the flat, however, she almost fell asleep. To make up for a mediocre main course, they had both had an exotic yet very filling pudding. And a second bottle of wine. They were taking their toll, those things and the evening in general. She was, quite suddenly, exhausted.

'Charlotte? We're home. Come on, sleepy, I'll see you to your door.'

She looked at him through half-closed eyes. We're

home. What a lovely idea, she thought sleepily. If only they were—home. *Together* . . .

There was no moon tonight, only the light of a lamp some distance away. But Curtis's profile, strong and finely carved, was perfectly visible . . . inviting. 'Just a minute.' Her voice came out huskily as she reached for him, drawing him towards her.

It was a mistake, getting involved like that while they were still in the car. Wasn't it? It started with her lips against his cheek, tracing the line of his jaw until, with a low moan, his mouth claimed hers. What began as a kiss turned into a good old-fashioned necking session, until in turn things changed again and they were straining for more bodily contact, not the easiest thing to achieve in the front seat of a car. Charlotte was arched against him, her breath coming in short gasps as his hands moved hungrily over the silky skin of her breasts beneath the thin material of her blouse.

The approach of another car, the arc of its headlights as it swung into the car park, had them pulling apart almost guiltily. The car stopped, its lights went out, a door slammed. Footsteps headed towards the building.

Curtis's voice cut through the darkness, his breathing was ragged, his words tinged with humour. 'I thought I was long past this sort of thing—in a car, for heaven's sake. I'm far too old!' His hand slid to the back of her neck, his fingers moving into her hair at the nape. 'Let's get indoors, my lovely. This is quite uncivilised.'

And finish what we've started. What *she* had started. No. She was tucking her blouse into her skirt, hardly able to credit the way she had encouraged all this. Being picked up in the headlights of a car had embarrassed her. Unlike Curtis, she didn't find it comical. Unlike Curtis, for her, the moment, the mood, had gone.

'I'll see myself in,' she said softly, reaching for the handle of the door.

His sharp intake of breath made her cringe. He was about to give her a telling off, and she deserved it. She was cross with herself; he surely must be cross with her.

If he were, it didn't show. 'Charlotte.' The word rendered her motionless. His hand reached out, caught hold of her chin, turned her to face him. She couldn't see his eyes very well, but she didn't need to. She knew exactly how they must look. 'Why?' he asked softly.

She answered with the truth, as far as it went. 'I'm sorry, Curtis, really I am. I'm shattered. It's two in the morning and——'

'And don't give me that. I've let you set the pace, Charlotte—I've done that all along. Think about it. But don't do this to me too often.'

She bit her lip, noting the warning in his last sentence.

'No games—I thought we agreed on that. In any case,' he added, letting her hear his smile, 'you're fighting a losing battle. I told you that some time ago. Not that you needed to be told. It's only a matter of time, Charlotte. You know that as well as I. We are going to be lovers. It's inevitable. Now come on, I'll see you safely to your door.'

Inevitable. Charlotte repeated the word to herself as she got ready for bed that night. It's inevitable.

Yes, yes, it was.

She didn't expect to hear from him the next day. Or on Friday. He had gone to Brighton on business, was staying overnight. His last words to her were to say that he would see her on Saturday.

Charlotte sat by the phone all Saturday morning. What had happened? Why hadn't he phoned? Maybe she should ring him? No. He had given her his private number long since but she'd never used it. Hadn't had occasion to until now. And now she was loath to ring him. What if he'd changed his mind, gone to his sister for the weekend?

At twelve-thirty she went out, very, very reluctantly. But she simply had to do some shopping. There was no food in the flat, and she was hungry. And what if he didn't ring? What did he have in mind? He'd said he would see her—but *when*? Where was the phone call to arrange things?

She wasn't gone long. On her return she waited again, becoming anxious. This wasn't like him. Why shouldn't she ring him, anyway? It wouldn't look as though she were chasing him, would it? No, not at this stage.

She tried his number, but there was no answer.

And then it dawned on her. It was Saturday. The gallery was open, maybe he was downstairs or in his office? She tried the number that would put her through to the offices.

'Mr Maxwell's office.'

Surprised, Charlotte gently replaced the receiver. She knew the voice. It was his secretary, the woman who had been off sick for several weeks. She hadn't expected any of the office staff to answer, not on a Saturday. There had been no point in talking to his secretary—what excuse could she have given for ringing, at a weekend?

When nothing had happened by the time she was due to leave for the church hall, she tried his private number again. It was nearly six o'clock, almost time to go. Geoffrey would be here shortly; they had to get to the hall early to allow time to talk with the rest of the cast, to change and make-up.

There was no answer. Like a fool she let the phone ring more than twenty times, hoping, hoping.

Maybe he'd had an accident?

It didn't bear thinking about.

Panic-stricken, she replaced the receiver carefully, keeping her eyes on it as if it knew something she didn't. Curtis, where *are* you?

Maybe he'd phoned while she was out? Maybe he'd been here? No, she hadn't been gone long. But if he had driven over here he'd have waited around a while, surely? No, he'd have phoned first, to check she was in.

Maybe they were at cross-purposes, having simply neglected to clarify things? 'I'll *see* you,' he'd said, not 'I'll ring you.'

That was it, it had to be. He must have meant that he'd pick her up after the play tonight. Satisfied that this was how it would be, Charlotte dashed into the bedroom and grabbed a dress just as Geoffrey rang the bell. She would take the dress with her, and her ordinary make-up, be ready to go out to eat when he came for her after the performance.

Curtis was there after the play finished. He announced his presence this time with a single red rose. Sandra brought it to Charlotte, again as she was removing her make-up.

'Well, Charlie, I must say I envy you.' Sandra wasn't smiling this time, she was merely interested. 'Does he know what this means,' she asked, handing over the rose, 'in the language of flowers?'

I love you, wasn't that what it meant? Wasn't it twelve red roses for friendship and a single one for that simple statement? 'I—I don't know,' Charlotte said honestly, looking at the perfect, velvety petals. 'I doubt it.' She meant that, too.

Sandra lowered her voice, not that there was any danger of their being overheard, the small room was overcrowded and there was too much chatter going on around them. 'He's outside,' she gestured towards the dressing-room door. 'I mean, he's waiting for you right there.'

'Oh! Er—Sandra, please would you tell him I'll be about five minutes?'

'With pleasure.' There was a smile now. 'Don't worry, I'll entertain him for you!'

When Charlotte emerged, Sandra was doing just that. She tactfully excused herself and left when Charlotte appeared.

'Curtis! I—thank you for this.' She looked at the flower she was holding. When he merely nodded, said nothing, she went on, 'I wondered what happened to you today, you didn't make it clear about——'

'I know, I'm sorry about that.' He seemed vaguely preoccupied, made no effort to kiss her or to take her hand. 'I wasn't sure exactly what my plans were until today. By the way, your performance tonight was even better than on Wednesday.'

Startled, she started laughing. 'You didn't sit through it again? I thought you'd just arrived. I tried ringing you at lunch-time and again around six tonight, but——'

'I'd left by then. I allowed time to stop off for a drink on the way here. I'm not alone, Charlotte, I brought my sister. I did try to ring you today, around one, but you weren't in. I thought you might like to come out to lunch with me and Chris. She's been with me all day.'

'You've brought your sister? She's *here*?' Charlie was delighted.

'She's waiting for us in the hall. I thought we'd all have supper. She's staying with me this weekend.'

'Oh, but I'm longing to meet her!' As Charlie began to move, Curtis caught hold of her arm.

'Just a minute, Charlotte. Wait.' There was an odd note in his voice. She turned to face him, frowning. 'There's—something I have to tell you first. Christine is blind.'

CHAPTER EIGHT

'BLIND?' Stunned, Charlotte parroted the word, watching the fleeting expression of pain on his face as she did do. 'Oh, Curtis, I—I had no idea! I'm—I'm so sorry! Why didn't you mention this before?'

He didn't answer that, he merely took her arm. 'Come on, as long as you've been told. Chris always insists I tell people before they meet her, she thinks they might be embarrassed otherwise.'

And she's right, Charlie thought. A feeling of unease settled inside her. Had she been introduced to Curtis's sister without having been warned, she would have been embarrassed at the discovery. She had never mixed with anyone who was blind before, but she felt certain that what they would want most of all would be for people to behave naturally with them, without inhibition or embarrassment.

Which was precisely how Charlie did behave.

Unfortunately, however, there was another shock in store for her. Curtis hadn't mentioned, either, that Chris was his twin, so the instant Charlie set eyes on her she was taken aback by their similarity.

'Why—my goodness, you two are so alike! You're beautiful Christine!' These were Charlotte's first words as she was introduced to Curtis's sister. She spoke without thinking, saying just what was in her mind. Chris was around five feet ten inches tall, standing proud, straight-backed, elegant in a midnight-blue velvet jacket with matching skirt. Her hair was exactly the same blonde as that of her twin except that there was no scattering of grey in it. It was pure, natural platinum blonde. Her eyes, too, were just like those of her brother, intensely blue, showing no sign whatever of their inability to see.

'Beautiful?' There it was again, a similarity in the way she laughed softly, just as Curtis did when he was really amused and was about to crack a joke. 'And alike? Well, that says a lot for you, doesn't it, Curtis?' She turned her head, for all the world as if she could see him. Only the fact that she looked generally and not specifically at him gave anything away. She could not, of course, achieve direct eye contact herself.

'And it tells me something about you, too.' Chris turned back to Charlotte, a smile of genuine amusement hovering around her mouth. 'You're biased! Anyhow,' she extended her hand, 'how do you do? I'm really happy to meet you, and I so enjoyed your performance! Curtis told me how splendid you were when he saw you on—Wednesday, wasn't it? So I asked him to bring me tonight. I love watching plays—if you see what I mean!'

That was all Charlie needed to be put completely at ease with Chris. With Chris but not with . . . Curtis wasn't himself, not quite, there was a certain tension about him. He had said nothing so far, was just standing, watching the exchange. He was smiling but the smile had not reached his eyes. Why? Why couldn't he relax? If Charlie could, he certainly should be able to.

She reached out, taking a firm hold of the proffered hand. 'Thank you. But as I said to Curtis the other day, this is hardly what you could call a night at the theatre. Believe me, this church hall is a very—er—basic sort of place.'

There was a nod, a shrug, as if Christine knew that full well but it didn't matter in the least. Then she giggled, lowering her voice. 'I didn't even notice how hard the seats were till the show was over—that's how entertained I was. I thought the play was very sad, Charlotte. I'm sure I laughed in all the wrong places, but people do, don't they, tend to laugh at what they're afraid of?'

'Yes. I think——'

'Excuse me, ladies,' at last Curtis spoke up, 'but do you think we could continue this discussion in the car?'

Which was just what they did. Charlotte and Chris dissected the play during the ride to—wherever they were going. Charlie, sitting next to Curtis and still holding on to her rose, was twisted round in her seat, nattering to his sister. They had liked one another instantly, and she was relieved to see that Curtis was himself again. He added his own comments about the moral of the play.

'And what will you do next?' asked Chris. 'Has the next play been chosen?'

'No. It won't be until September. We don't do anything during July and August, too many people go away on holiday. And I won't necessarily be in the next one, I certainly won't have the lead. Everyone has to have a turn.'

'But you'll let me know, won't you, whether you're in it? I'd like to come and see it if you are. I'll give you my phone number later. And, Charlotte, the next time Curtis comes to the Cotswolds, do come with him. I have a nice little flat there, just two bedrooms, but we can work something out.'

'You live alone?'

'Sort of. Hasn't Curtis told you? Oh. Well, I live in a home for the blind—but in a flat of my own. It's in one of the wings. The Maxwell wing,' she added proudly. 'Curtis paid for it to be built, it's an extension of the main building, which was once a private residence, and it has several completely self-contained flats in it.'

Charlotte was looking at Curtis as Chris continued. She was talking about her neighbours now, about how some of them were partially sighted, why some were better off in the main building, and how some of the others, those who were able to cope, preferred to live in the flats.

Curtis was silent again, his eyes on the road.

Charlotte was feeling a touch of resentment. He paid for the extension? The Maxwell wing? Why hadn't he told her about his sister, why hadn't he told her any of this?

They were in Mayfair, circling the block which housed the Maxwell Gallery. Curtis brought the car to a halt in a small, cobbled courtyard at the back of the building. There was an entrance directly into his flat from here. Charlotte was keen to see his home, it meant she would also get to see his private collection of paintings.

'If you'll excuse me, girls, I'll go and see to our supper.' They were all having a drink in the living-room when Curtis excused himself.

'Want any help?' Charlotte offered.

'No, I can cope. It's very basic, believe me! You stay here and entertain Chris.'

Alone, Charlotte turned to his sister. 'You have the advantage over me. I don't know anything about you. What do you do with yourself, how do you pass your time?'

'Oh, I keep quite busy, actually. I work on the switchboard at the home three or four days a week, depending. I also do some counselling work, you know, with people who haven't been blind for long, trying to help them adjust, to encourage them, to make them believe that one is not totally useless just because one can't see. We've also been invited to some schools in the area, to give talks. I suppose I could call it social education—talking to children about what it's like being blind. It's quite interesting, really. You should hear some of the questions they ask!'

'Like what?' Charlie was impressed. Chris had meant it when she said she kept herself busy.

'Like whether blind people dream, whether they dream in colour. Oh, yes, I've also given a couple of talks on the radio, did one a few weeks ago, actually. The local radio, I mean.

'And of course I read Braille,' she went on, 'and I sometimes spend time making cassette recordings, stories for others to listen to, those who haven't yet learned to read themselves.'

'Well, you really do keep busy!'

Christine smiled, a smile of satisfaction. It faded a moment later. Quietly she asked, 'You didn't know any of this? Hadn't Curtis told you anything at all about me?'

Hesitating, Charlotte answered carefully. 'Very little.'

'Come on, Charlotte, you didn't even know we were twins. Tell me the truth.' She was smiling again, but it was a wry little smile. 'Had he even told you he had a sister before tonight?'

'Of course!' But she had had to ask, hadn't she? She'd had to ask who Chris was.

A little later they were all seated at a circular dining-table, eating a crunchy salad with cheese, warm French bread and a superb red wine taken from the rack in Curtis's kitchen. Not surprisingly the flat was masculine-orientated, the furniture in the living-room being a little sombre, predominantly made from tan-coloured leather. But it was a nice place, very much so, luxurious and beautifully furnished, although it wasn't quite what Charlotte had expected—where was his collection of paintings?

It was when they moved back from the dining-room to the living-room that Christine's blindness became most apparent. Without Curtis by her side to guide her, she had to feel her way around.

'I haven't got this place perfectly sussed out yet,' she said. 'Curtis always tells me if he's moved something, but he tends to do that fairly often and I sometimes forget!'

'That's because you don't come here often enough,' her brother admonished. 'Nothing's changed since you were here last.'

Chris turned to Charlotte as they sat down. 'My darling brother is very bossy. But you must know that already.'

Forgetting herself, Charlotte nodded, grinning. Then, because she felt instinctively that the other girl would appreciate it, she added, 'Sorry, Chris. I did acknowledge what you said but for the moment I forgot you couldn't see me. I was nodding.'

'And grinning,' Curtis put in.

Christine laughed delightedly, her own acknowledgement a graceful inclination of her head. 'You'll get used to me,' she told Charlotte.

I hope so, she thought, her eyes going of their own accord to Curtis. I hope I get the chance to get used to you, to get to know you really well.

'What was I saying?' asked Chris. 'Oh, yes—about *him*! Brother dear, would you fill up my wine-glass, please? Mm—about the bossiness. If he isn't forcing his presence on me at home, he's pestering me to come here. Fetches me, of course, as if I'm not capable of getting to the railway station and getting on a train. I have a guide dog, you know, a marvellous creature I call Della, so I can get around very easily. But Curtis insists on fetching me and——'

'Then I drag you to the opera or a play or a musical.' Her brother laughed at her. 'And you love it!'

Charlie watched in fascination, interested in the banter, touched by the warmth, the love, between them. It was unmistakable. When she said she had to go home, simply because she couldn't keep her eyes open any longer, it was with a pang of regret. 'I hope I see you again soon, Chris. It's been lovely.'

The older woman got to her feet, both hands outstretched this time. Charlotte moved over to her quickly, taking the hands in hers. 'I hope so too, Charlotte. Now hang on a minute, we must exchange telephone numbers. Tell me yours, I'll remember it. I have a fantastic memory for numbers.'

Charlie gave her the number and wrote Christine's number in her diary in her handbag. 'Tell me, do you prefer to be called Chris or Christine?'

'I prefer Chris. And you? Charlie or Charlotte? I'd like to call you Charlie, I believe others do, but Curtis thinks that's dreadful!'

'I don't mind either way.'

'Well, I do! I'm one of those old-fashioned types who likes a woman to be a woman,' said Curtis, his intense blue gaze moving to Charlotte. 'To look and feel and smell and sound like one. And to be addressed as one.'

'Do you mind?' Chris was looking at Charlotte, her hands moving to her upper arms, to her cheeks. Charlotte smiled, waited, minded not in the least that Chris wanted to touch her face, to get an idea of how she looked.

'And I'm almost as tall as you.'

Chris nodded. 'And more beautiful, I'm sure. Curtis has told me about your glorious hair and about your eyes, what an unusual colour they are, how big and expressive——'

'Chris! I think you've said more than enough. I must take Charlotte home now. Right now!' Her twin was laughing, shaking his head.

'Nooo! Tell me more, more. I like it!' It was another ten minutes before Charlie got away. Chris didn't say more, but the teasing went on between all of them.

Once inside the Jaguar, Charlie turned immediately to Curtis. 'Why didn't you tell me about her? I mean, before tonight?'

He shrugged, not looking at her because he was reversing the car. 'It didn't occur to me that I should, before you met her,'

'But—but what about the rest of it?'

'The rest of it?'

'The home—the wing you put on. I mean, that's a pretty wonderful——'

'Nonsense! I did that for Chris.'

'*That's* nonsense! What about all the other people who live in it?'

His voice was clipped, startling her into silence. 'Leave it alone, Charlotte. That's something I don't choose to talk about, any more than I volunteer to people that my sister is blind.'

She looked down at her hands. People? Was that all she was to him? One of the general public or something? Her eyes moved to the red rose, lying on the dashboard where she had left it earlier.

'Did you like her?' Curtis asked at length, his tone reflecting his thoughtfulness.

'You know I did.'

'Yes,' he agreed, his pleasure apparent now. 'And she thought you adorable, I can tell. She and I are very close.'

Which was true. But in any case, Curtis had very strong instincts, was sensitive to people. Even with strangers. He had been able to read her moods right from the start, regardless of her trying to disguise her feelings.

She turned to look at him as he drove, her heart contracting then flipping over wildly.

She waited a second or two until she could trust herself to sound normal when she spoke. 'I've been longing to ask you, but I didn't like to in front of Chris, where is your art collection? Mr Grant's spoken of it with a great deal of envy,' she added laughingly. She had wanted to ask this when she was in his flat, had been astonished to see only a regular number of paintings dotted around the place. But she hadn't asked because it didn't seem tactful in front of Chris. Chris had never seen and would never be able to see her brother's collection.

'It's at the house. My home.' There was a momentary pause. 'Well, no, the house. I should say the house, I was right first time.'

Charlie's eyes closed for a moment. 'Do I have to ask or are you going to tell me?' What else was she going to learn about him tonight?

Curtis appeared not to know what she meant for a moment. 'Oh, haven't I told you about the house?'

'No.' To herself she added, it's just another detail you've omitted to mention. How many more shocks was she in for tonight?

'I'm talking about my childhood home, a big rambling place in Buckinghamshire.'

'But—but who lives there?' Charlie was trying to put it all together. Chris lived in the Cotswolds, he lived in Mayfair, and his parents were both dead, he'd told her that much.

'Just a housekeeper and a couple of staff. And the paintings,' he added, his easy smile, his words, causing her eyebrows to go up.

'And that's it?'

'That's it. Except for me and Chris, when we're there. We sometimes spend a weekend there—if we're not at her place or if there's nothing she wants to see in London. She loves the house, and you see, she knows every nook and cranny of it. She remembers every detail——'

It was happening again. For some reason, Charlie had assumed that Chris had been blind from birth. 'So—she *was* sighted, once?'

There was a delay before he answered and when the answer came it was with that unspoken message that he didn't want to discuss this any further. 'Yes. Until she was ten. And then—she was involved in an accident.'

Charlotte bit back what she wanted to say. She wanted to say, 'How awful for her,' but she checked herself because it simply wasn't necessary. Curtis already knew how awful it had been for his sister. And the message had come across loud and clear: I don't want to talk about the accident.

Nothing was said for a moment or two. They were turning into the courtyard outside Charlie's flat.

'I'll take you to the house as soon as I can.' Curtis swung the car into a space, switched off the engine. 'You want to see my collection, right?'

'Right!'

'It belongs to me and Chris, actually. And you needn't have worried about mentioning it in front of her. She's familiar with almost all the works, most of them have been in the family for years and years. She remembers them. Any additions I've made to the collection, I've described to her in detail. She knows them all, she even knows what's hanging where. As I said, she knows that house inside out, which is why we keep it on. Now then, about your seeing this collection . . .' He reached for a switch, turned off his lights. 'It'll cost you . . .'

'Oh, yes?' Charlotte was laughing now. 'That's not your style, Curtis!'

'Ah, but it is!' He was reaching for her, his hands sliding under her hair as he brought her face close to his. 'And I demand payment in advance.'

She paid, willingly.

A moment later they were pulling apart, not because anyone could see them but because it was the only sensible thing to do. One kiss was all it took. They were both on fire within seconds. 'You'd better go,' she said reluctantly. 'Chris . . .'

'Yes. I don't like to leave her alone in the flat for too long, she's not all that familiar with its layout.' Curtis didn't let go of her, though. He kissed her again and again, finally moving away from her with an effort. 'What am I,' he asked wryly, 'some sort of masochist? Charlotte——'

'I know, I know.' She, too, was having difficulty

regaining control. God, how she wanted him! Tonight. Now. Now, when it wasn't possible . . . 'Will I see you tomorrow?'

Curtis ran a hand across his forehead, his fingers raking through the thick blondness of his hair. 'Dammit, I'll have some packing to do. And I'll be driving Chris home first.'

Packing: that was all she heard. 'Packing?' Charlotte spoke in a small voice, her disappointment almost making her mute. This was the worst shock of them all. 'Where—where are you going?

'To New York. Late tomorrow. I'm——'

'*New York!*' Physically and mentally unable to take this calmly, she pulled away, almost accusing him. 'Oh, *Curtis*! Why didn't you tell me before? How many more times am I going to hear myself saying that tonight?'

'Darling!' He pulled her close, distressed by her outburst. 'Hey, relax now. I'm sorry, I'm sorry. Really. It—I didn't know about this myself till this morning, honestly. I mean about New York. There are only a few members of my staff whom I would trust to go buying for me, two of them are on holiday and two of them have got this 'flu bug that's going around. The second chap fell victim yesterday. Charlotte, I didn't mean to upset you.' Then, softly, his lips against her brow, 'But I'm glad you are upset. I'll miss you, too. I'll get back as fast as I can.'

She nestled against him, slipping her hand into his, loving the feel of him, the masculine scent of him, the warmth of him. 'The preview—the Licer exhibition. The preview's on Friday. You'll miss it.'

'No, I'll be there. I'll be back by then.'

'You will?' She stirred, looking at him, feeling happier now.

'I'll make sure of it.' Curtis smiled, a gentle smile, before kissing her good night.

CHAPTER NINE

THE single red rose was looking a little sorry for itself by Tuesday, decidedly so on Wednesday. It was in a slender, crystal single-bud vase, in the shade on the window-sill in Charlie's kitchen. Each morning and evening, she looked at it.

It was dying by Thursday.

Knowing that Curtis was on the other side of the world, or as good as, was like living with a dull pain which she knew would go away but which bothered her enormously in the meantime. Sunday to Friday—just six days. No, five. She would see him on Friday. He had said he would make it to the preview of Fernando Licer's work.

How slowly the time passed, how empty the days seemed! There were no rehearsals, even, to distract her; the drama society wouldn't be meeting again until September.

The rose was stone dead by Friday.

Before leaving for work, Charlotte stood and looked at it. *Had* Curtis known its symbolism when he gave it to her, had he? They had telephones in America, didn't they? He hadn't phoned.

She told herself he was probably too busy, maybe moving around a lot. He was on a buying trip; yes, he was probably moving around from place to place. And then there was the time difference to make things even more inconvenient . . .

Reluctantly, she plucked the flower from the vase and threw it into the waste bin, hoping there was no symbolism here and now, no omen in the fact that it had breathed its last breath today. Had he missed her as much as she had missed him? Had he? Was he longing to see her? Was her absence an ache inside his breast?

She went back to her bedroom, checked her appearance in the mirror. In a coffee-and-cream checked suit, matching cream-coloured blouse, she looked just right. The preview was opening at six o'clock and would last a couple of hours. The press would be there, journalists from the art world and from two or three national dailies. She had organised everything; all the gallery staff had been instructed not to mention the source of the loan of *The Lady in White*. Just that one painting. And still she didn't know the reason for this. Understanding Curtis Maxwell, she had to admit, was not the easiest thing in the world.

Her reflection pleased her. Maybe she should change, take the suit off and carry it to work? She wanted to look fresh, crisp, for the preview.

For Curtis.

Laughing at herself, she left the flat at once. Barring accidents, she'd look just fine this evening.

By seven o'clock Charlie was almost frantic, not that she allowed herself to show it. The rooms of the gallery were buzzing, people were still moving around from painting to painting, helping themselves to the cheese and wine which had been set up for them on a table. People came and went.

But Curtis wasn't among them.

All sorts of things were going through her mind: postponement, pressure of work, *plane crashes*! Where was he? Why hadn't he turned up?

'So where is our illustrious Mr Maxwell?' Linda, Charlie's secretary, voiced the question which was going through the other girl's mind. Although Charlotte hadn't spoken of her relationship with Curtis, other than to say she was seeing him, Linda knew very well the effect Curtis Maxwell was having on her boss.

'I don't know—I just don't know! He's been buying in New York, was supposed to be flying back today . . .'

Linda smiled reassuringly. 'Hey, relax, will you? You know what it's like with airlines. He's probably been delayed, that's all.'

And then, suddenly, there he was. Across the crowded room, Charlotte spotted him. 'Some enchanted evening' . . . She thought of the song to which the line belonged. 'You may see a stranger . . .'

No stranger, this! It was only then, as her heart began to race frantically at the sight of him, that she realised she loved him. Already she was moving towards him, her smile eager, brilliant. I love you, *I love you, Curtis*! She said it over and over to herself, laughing aloud because she should have known it before, laughing because now he had seen her and she knew with equal certainty that he felt the same way.

He loved her!

He was moving towards her as rapidly as he could among the throng of people. They met in the middle of the room and he took her in his arms, oblivious to all that was happening around him, oblivious to everything but her. Almost hugging the breath from her, he told her how very much he'd missed her, '. . . the most miserable days of my life, Charlotte.'

'For me, too,' she whispered.

'I've driven straight from the airport, darling. I——' That was all there was time for. Curtis was immediately collared by a journalist wanting to know more about the six paintings he had loaned, and did he know who owned *The Lady in White*?

'Yes, I do,' he admitted. 'But I'm not at liberty to say. Sorry.'

Charlotte moved away and left him to it.

It was almost eight-thirty before they got away, turned nine when they reached her flat. She went immediately into the kitchen to put the kettle on, glancing at the empty vase on her window-sill and laughing at herself for the doubts she'd had that morning. No, there had been no omen. Curtis was as much in love with her as she was with him.

'Are you hungry? I've got——' She called over her shoulder, stopping in mid-sentence as long, strong arms closed around her waist.

Curtis turned her round to face him. 'You bet I am! But I don't want anything to eat.'

Again they were kissing, as they had as soon as they'd got into his car a short time ago. 'Enough!' Charlotte protested laughingly. 'I need——'

'Never, never enough!'

'A cup of coffee,' she finished. 'Darling man, honestly, I'm gasping.'

'Me, too.' The smile was roguish now.

'For a *cuppa*! Kindly remember how hard I've been working all day. Give a girl a chance, hmm? Make yourself useful. Switch on the lamps, close the curtains.'

He gave her a bow. 'I like the sound of that, I like, I like! Maybe I'll put on some music, too.'

And he did, quietly. They sat on the settee, drinking coffee and talking. He told her about his trip, but only briefly. Soon, inevitably, she was in his arms again. His mouth was on hers, its gentle pressure parting her lips. She was crushed against the hardness of his chest, able to feel the rapid beat of his heart against her breasts. Her hands were inside the jacket of his suit, exploring the contours of his back against the silk of his shirt.

'Curtis . . .' He slipped off his jacket, eased her back against the cusions, covering her face with tiny kisses, then letting his lips linger on her neck, nestling in the hollow at the base of her throat.

Charlotte's pulses were pounding, everything in her was crying out for him when his weight shifted so that he was on top of her, his own need exciting her,

arousing her, even further. She made no protest when
he began to open the buttons of her blouse. The time
was right now.

For them.

For her. At long last, for her. There had been no
other man. Not like this.

'Curtis . . .' Her slender fingers closed around his
wrist, halting them. 'I——' She hardly knew how to
tell him. She was almost twenty-four years old, for
heaven's sake. 'There's—a danger that you, I mean
that I—I might disappoint you.'

There was a frown before understanding dawned in
his eyes. With a groan he gathered her close, held her
tenderly against the solid wall of his chest.

'I love you,' she whispered. 'Oh, I love you so much!
Take me to bed, Curtis, make love to me. Now. Please!'

She was lifted into his arms and they were at the
door of the living-room when the front-door bell rang.
Charlotte looked across the short space of the hall,
unable to believe what she had heard. Curtis lowered
his head, his lips against her ear. 'Leave it! Ignore it.
They'll go away.'

The bell rang again.

'It's no use,' she groaned. 'It'll be Geoffrey, I just
know it. He won't go away. He'll be able to hear the
music. He'll know I'm in.'

Curtis set her on her feet, muttering something very
uncomplimentary about her neighbour while she
hastily re-buttoned her blouse.

Sure enough, it was Geoffrey. 'Hi, Charlie! I
wonder if——' He broke off, his eyes going over her
shoulder. She turned. The door of the living-room
was still open and that was where Curtis was,
standing by the fireplace, his back to them.

'I'm sorry.' Geoffrey spoke quietly to Charlotte,
then more loudly so Curtis could hear, 'Sorry to
interrupt, Mr Maxwell.'

There was a grunt from the living-room.

Charlotte blushed furiously, making matters worse. Geoffrey's eyes narrowed for a second, then he looked horrified. 'Oh! I'm—Charlie, I'll go. I'm sorry, I didn't mean——'

'It's all right.' She got control of herself, even managed a smile. 'What did you want?'

'Some teabags.'

'*Teabags?*'

'Yes, I've got company myself and I haven't——'

'Oh, yes?'

'My parents.' He relaxed a little. 'I wasn't expecting them. Mum never drinks coffee, I drink nothing but. If I'd known they were coming—but the deli closes at nine and I didn't——'

'It's all right,' she said again. Anything to silence his rambling. Anything to get rid of him! 'Don't worry about it, Geoffrey. Hang on, I'll get a few and stick them in a bag for you.'

'I wouldn't have——'

'I know.' Her voice was tinged with impatience now. 'It's *all right*. Just wait there.' But before she could move, Curtis was upon them. His jacket was slung over his shoulder, his face was like thunder and he was walking so fast that both Charlotte and Geoffrey automatically stepped aside.

'Curtis!' She couldn't believe her eyes. He was leaving!

'Mr Maxwell——'

'I'm sorry, Charlotte.' Curtis ignored her neighbour. 'I'll explain. When I can.'

And he was gone. *Gone.*

Almost as stunned as she was, Geoffrey, too, watched as Curtis turned the corner at the end of the corridor. He was the first to recover. 'Grief, what's up with him?'

If only she knew!

'Charlie, I don't know what to say, I didn't mean to chase him away!'

She smiled, a mirthless smile. How he flattered himself! As if *he* could—'I'll get the teabags.'

By the time she did so, her hands were trembling. Geoffrey took them from her, retreated gratefully, leaving her to wonder what on earth she'd done wrong. Dear God, he had looked so *angry!*

But why? What had she done? Had she said something . . .?

She walked back into the living-room and burst into tears. She knew what she'd done wrong. She'd deceived herself. She'd seen in his face, his reaction upon seeing her tonight, what she'd wanted to see.

It hadn't been real.

Worse, she'd told him she loved him.

But he hadn't said a word about love himself, had he?

Fool. *Fool.* He had told her that first weekend he would never marry. And she had worn her heart on her sleeve, put her feelings into words. He must have expected her to expect . . . to expect more than he was prepared to give, perhaps. *She had frightened him off!*

Sobbing, she thought of Edward Grant's words, 'Nobody's immune to love.'

Oh, how wrong he was! Wrong, wrong, wrong! At least, if Curtis Maxwell were capable of falling in love, it wasn't going to be with her.

It was midnight, precisely midnight, when she dragged herself to bed. Half an hour later she was up again. Sleep was impossible, out of the question. 'I'll explain,' he'd said, 'when I can.' When I can? What did that mean?

Charlotte sat, crying again, turning her mind inside out in an effort to understand. That he could have walked out when they were on the verge of making love . . . He didn't love her, but he wanted her. That was one thing she was not mistaken about. How could he have left when he did?

And why? *Why?*

Her despair turned to anger. Dabbing at her eyes
with a tissue, she reached for the phone. He could
damn well explain himself now, right now!

Five minutes later she put down the receiver, having
let the phone ring all that time. Either he was sound
asleep or he wasn't answering his telephone.

It was turned one o'clock when the doorbell pierced
the silence of the flat. Her head snapped up. She
hadn't heard the sound of a car. Or maybe she had
heard the sound of several. She knew who it was
without a shadow of a doubt. Even Geoffrey didn't
come pestering her at one in the morning.

Nevertheless, she took a peep through the spyhole
in her front door. Opening the door, she retreated into
the living-room, saying nothing. She didn't know
what to say. At the sight of him, her anger had
suddenly turned into fear. Suddenly she knew what
was coming, what he had come back to tell her. He
looked shattered, in need of a shave, dishevelled. And
she, she looked like a woman who was about to face
the gallows, shoulders slumped, eyes swollen.

Curtis flinched at the sight of her. 'Charlotte, I—
I'm sorry. I owe you an explanation.'

It was seconds before she could answer him, she
couldn't even look at him. 'Yes.'

'May I sit down?'

'Of course.' She lowered herself into a chair, his
formality almost terrifying her. She knew, she knew
what was coming.

'I've been driving around,' he went on quietly. 'I
needed to think. I came back and I—I saw your light
was still on. Charlotte, I've come back to say
goodbye.'

CHAPTER TEN

NUMBLY, Charlotte nodded. She had known it, but the words stunned her just the same. She was too shocked for bitterness, too shocked to feel anything. 'Are you . . . are you going to tell me why?'

'Because I can't handle it. Because it isn't fair to you. This. Us.'

She looked at him then, she looked hard and long. 'I haven't the faintest idea what you mean.'

This was no easier for him than it was for her. 'I mean it's no use. It's pointless, we're on a road to nowhere.'

'Pointless.' She picked up on the word, not realising she'd voiced it. So she had been right in her thinking: he was assuming she would make demands on him. 'I've never asked you for anything, Curtis.' Her head came up, pride to the fore. 'We're right together, you can't deny it. And I mean in every respect, not just . . . You want me, I want you, so what do you mean, it's pointless?'

He looked away. 'I can't marry you, Charlotte.'

'I don't remember asking you to.'

'You or anyone else,' he added, as though he hadn't heard her. 'It wouldn't be fair.'

Charlotte's eyes closed of their own volition. She couldn't deny to herself what she was denying to him. To be married to this man would be, for her, the ultimate fulfilment. To work at his side, help him, wake up every morning beside him, love him, to look after and to be looked after, to have his children . . .

She couldn't speak, couldn't utter a sound.

'You love me,' he went on. 'I knew it before you did. When I saw you at the gallery this evening, I knew it for certain then, and I knew it had to finish, because I realised then how very deeply you felt. But I couldn't resist . . . and I had no way of knowing . . . of knowing what you told me tonight, just before . . . Believe it or not, I'm grateful to Geoffrey Hemmings. It was while you were talking to him that I came to my senses, realised what I'd almost done to you. It would have been an abuse, Charlotte. In those minutes while I was alone, I realised how wrong it would be of me to take advantage like that. You see tonight, all of it, has been—overwhelming.

'I've never felt about any woman the way I feel about you, I hope you'll believe that. I don't want an affair with you, Charlotte. Oh, I thought that would be enough. Right up until tonight, I thought it would be enough. But I've discovered you mean more to me than that. With you it would have to be all or nothing. I've got to make you understand. You see, my time, my life, is not wholly mine to give.'

A new wave of fear clutched at her heart. What was he *saying*? 'Curtis! Oh, Curtis, you're not—ill, are you?'

'No.' He closed his eyes, rubbing his knuckles over them tiredly, cruelly. 'No, I'm not ill, it's nothing like that. I'm just—living with something for which I can never forgive myself, from which I'll never be free.'

In the face of her silence, he added, simply, 'It's Chris.'

'Chris? What—what about her?'

With a look of pure agony, he said, 'I was the cause of her accident when she was little. I am the reason she's blind.'

Charlotte called upon all her acting abilities. She would not, would *not* allow him to see the shock she felt on hearing this. He was suffering enough without her adding to it. 'I can't believe that.'

'Well, you'd better!' Curtis snapped at her harshly, shooting to his feet, advancing on her as though he intended to shake the life out of her. Then he stopped dead, turning his back on her. 'I'm sorry.' He gestured towards the bottles and glasses on a shelf in the recess by the fireplace. 'I need a drink. Will you have one?'

'No.' She waited, silently, until he had poured himself a drink.

He still wasn't looking at her. Charlotte's heart went out to him as he struggled to explain. 'We were ten years old. It was during the school holidays. We were out riding, not too far from the house in Bucks. We were both good, capable riders. We came to a fence, nothing that was too ambitious for either of us. I took the fence, but Chris's horse refused to jump. I teased her, jeered at her. You've met her, Charlotte, you'll believe me when I tell you she had as much personality at ten as she has today. She rose to the challenge. I called her a chicken, laughed at her. She settled the horse, went back and rode at the fence. At the last second, her horse refused it again and . . . and threw her.'

There was a long, long pause. It seemed to Charlotte as if she had to wait hours for him to finish. But of course she knew already what he was about to say.

'Chris was unconscious for three days. She had hit the ground head first. When she came to, she was blind. There was no hope for repair, recovery. My father was a wealthy man, my parents took her to the best specialists in the world. It was hopeless.'

Silence again.

Charlotte's mind was working frantically, her mouth trying to form words of comfort. She wasn't thinking about herself, only of him. 'It was an accident,' she said at length.

'It needn't have happened. I goaded her into it.'

'It was an *accident*! And what are you telling me?' she went on, deliberately putting scorn into her voice. 'That you'll never marry because of this? This is what you meant, I suppose, when you said you'd never marry because you had too many commitments? You meant Chris.'

'Stop that!' Curtis rounded on her furiously. 'How the hell can I expect you to understand? Yes, that is precisely what I meant. I *am* committed to her, I owe her, I want to look after her to the very best of my ability. I want to spend as much time with her as I'm able to. She needs me, she needs me more than anyone else possibly could.'

Oh, God! she thought. Oh, God, he's wrong about that, very wrong! But I can't tell him so. Coming from me, he'd never even begin to believe it!

Wretched, feeling helpless, trapped because of her own admission of love, she had placed herself in the position where she couldn't begin to help him, to make him see how wrong he was, how he was continuing after all these years to punish himself for what had been, purely and simply, an accident.

In that moment, Charlotte knew how pointless it was. Pointless. Curtis had used precisely the right word. She could see now how right he'd been. She could see, now, that she would get nowhere with him. If she tried to point out how wrong he was in his thinking, he'd put it all down to her having an ulterior motive, selfish reasons of her own. She'd said she loved him. He knew what she'd been hoping for in her heart of hearts. Despite her earlier attempt at nonchalance, her implication that she would be his lover with no strings attached, he *knew*. She never had been able to fool him when it came to what she was really feeling.

But she had to try, for his sake, she had to. 'Curtis, you're wrong!' She cast about in her mind, wondering how best to tackle this. 'Does Chris know the way you think, does she know of the way you're prepared to deny yourself?'

'Don't be ridiculous! Don't you think her life's

tough enough? Do you think I want to make her feel she's a liability or something? In any case, I'm denying myself nothing. This is how I want things to be.'

'Do you?' Charlotte got to her feet, stood in front of him and looked straight into his eyes. She was about to ask him a question, the answer to which was vital. 'You never did get round to saying quite what your feelings for me are, Curtis. Oh, you've implied respect and you said you've never felt about anyone the way you feel about me. What does that mean, exactly? Will you be honest, straightforward with me? Are you in love with me?'

His gaze didn't waver. His eyes were locked on to hers, blue, clear, hiding nothing. 'No, Charlotte, it doesn't go that far. I'm not in love with you.'

She took it bravely, the truth, the harsh reality. She nodded slowly, accepting, her shoulders lifting slightly. 'But I love you, so let me try to help you, let me try for the sake of the woman you might fall in love with, one day. Nobody's immune to love, Curtis. Not even you, much as you might not welcome it. So listen to me, believe what I tell you. If Chris had the slightest inkling of what you've said to me tonight, she would be appalled. She is a capable, independent woman. Certainly she needs you in her life, you're her brother, her twin. But she doesn't need you to that extent, to the extent where you have to spend nearly every weekend with her! Can't you see how warped your thinking is? How subjective? With my own ears I heard her protest that you inflict your company on her too much. Oh, she was half laughing, because she didn't want to hurt your feelings, but she *meant* it. I know she did——'

'You *know* she did?' He was unmoved, totally unconvinced. As she had known he would be. 'Is that a fact, Charlotte? It seems you know my sister better than I know her myself!'

And still she tried, for his sake. 'Maybe I do. I can see things you can't——'

'You can see what you want to see!'

'No, no! You're not helping Chris, believe me, you're not. All you're doing is trying to alleviate your feeling of guilt, a feeling which shouldn't be there in the first place! And what of her? There are some things in life which she is never likely to have, children for one. And you're denying yourself that, too. Curtis, you can't swap places with her, much as you'd like to! Don't you think it would make her happy to see you settled, to see you living normally, having a family——'

Even as she was saying this, she realised how she was negating the good she was trying to do. His eyebrows had risen, a look of pure cynicism was on his face. Then to her dismay, to her disgust he shook his head, as though he felt sorry for her. 'Don't look at me like that!' she protested. 'I know what you're thinking. You think I'm being subjective now.'

'You'd deny it?'

'Yes! No. Well, maybe I am, a little. I love you, Curtis. I'm not about to apologise for that, but it doesn't detract from the logic of what I'm trying to tell you.'

He seemed to have stopped listening. He swallowed what was left of his drink, finished what he had come back to say. 'I came to say goodbye. I'm sorry, Charlotte. Believe me, I am sorry.'

Within seconds he was gone. 'Curtis!' She was on her feet, going after him the instant she realised his intention. 'Curtis, wait! Please!'

The front door closed.

Charlie stopped in her tracks. She was in her dressing-gown. Besides, to run after him would do no good. He had gone. And, this time, he would not be back.

She stood motionless, utterly bewildered by all that

had happened. The entire evening seemed unreal to her now. She was in a state of shock. Just a few short hours ago she had been happier than she'd ever been. Then, suddenly, *wham*!

Curtis Maxwell had gone from her life as dramatically as he had entered it. Quickly, shockingly. That was how he had won her heart in a matter of weeks. And that was how he had left, leaving that same heart broken.

CHAPTER ELEVEN

'CHARLIE, what on earth's the matter? Are you ill?'

It was ten minutes to ten, Monday morning. Charlotte had never been this late for work in all the time she'd been at the gallery. But then she'd never been as short of sleep as she was now, had never had such a terrible weekend.

She hadn't cried again, she hadn't done anything much. There had been such a finality about Curtis's goodbye to her on Friday night, it had left her feeling stunned, wrung out, helpless.

And loving him.

But he didn't love her, so that was that. For him, it didn't go beyond the physical. She had to face these things, she had been telling herself all weekend that she had to adjust. She had also told herself it would only be a matter of time, that Curtis Maxwell had been in her life for only a few weeks, that she could surely forget him.

But oh, what a vast difference he had made to her life during those weeks! What a difference he had wrought in her! What had happened to the girl who was uninterested in men, the girl who had been perfectly happy with her life just as it was? She had thought herself a career girl, one who might or might not marry at some distant and nebulous point in the future. She hadn't needed men, hadn't needed that scene, as she had once put it to Curtis.

What irony! She had told him so adamantly, believing herself sincere. She *had* been sincere. And yet ... yet even then, even as she'd said the words, she had been in love with him. She had, she realised now, fallen in love with him during that very first time they'd had lunch. On sight, perhaps, even as he'd been rude to her that day in his office.

What did it matter, how, where or when? The damage was done. Regardless of what she told herself, she knew she would not forget him in a hurry. She couldn't wave a magic wand and become once again the contented girl she had been. Curtis had changed her irrevocably, had made her want different things from life, had made her think in terms of permanence and sharing and . . . Oh, God, she had to stop this! If she were going to hang on to her sanity, she had to stop thinking like this.

If only there were someone she could talk to!

She looked at her secretary, wishing she could talk things over with her. But she couldn't. It wasn't on, given all the circumstances. She couldn't discuss one of the benefactors of the art school with another member of staff, couldn't discuss the man's private life, his sister and what had happened when they were children.

Nor could she discuss things with Chris, though her first instinct had been to telephone her. She had wanted very much to do that, to tell Chris that Curtis had finished with her, and why. But how on earth could she? It would hurt Chris deeply, terribly, and it wouldn't alter Curtis's way of thinking. It wouldn't make him love her. It would change nothing at all. It was over, *over*, and no amount of wishful thinking, no amount of discussion with Linda, Chris or anyone else, would alter that fact.

'No, I'm O.K.' She took off her jacket, draped it on the hanger which lived on the back of the office door. The July weather was being unpredictable, mixed, on some days there was sunshine followed by rain followed by more sunshine. It was such that the sensible thing was to wear a sundress and carry a jacket and a brolly. 'I only slept for a couple of hours last night.'

Linda was staring at her. 'You look awful. What's happened?'

Charlotte shook her head.

'It's something to do with Curtis Maxwell, isn't it?'

With a shrug, Charlie nodded, avoiding Linda's eyes. There was only so much she could tell her, just the bare facts. 'It's over, Linda. He finished with me on Friday night.'

'Over?' The younger girl was incredulous. 'On Friday? But I thought—I was so certain . . .'

When Linda left the sentence unfinished, it was more than Charlotte could resist. 'What? What did you think?'

Linda shifted awkwardly. 'Well, I—the way you greeted each other at the preview, right in front of everyone, the way he looked at you, and you at him. Charlie, I know you're head over heels in love with the man. I've known it for some time. He swept you off your feet, right from the word go. And I—I'd have sworn you'd had the same effect on him. I'd have sworn he was as crazy about you.'

Charlie deliberately made her voice crisp, started rummaging in a drawer as she spoke. 'Then it just goes to show, appearances can be deceiving.'

Tactfully, Linda left it at that. She started typing, determined not to add to her boss's troubles in any way that could be avoided. 'By the way, Mr Grant's out for a couple of hours, he's in the school, in a meeting with the Principal.'

The news came as a relief to Charlotte. The art school had broken up for the holidays, actually, but there was a skeleton staff working.

Perhaps if she threw herself into her work, by the time Mr Grant came back she would look normal. She would work late tonight, to make up for the hour she'd lost and because—because suddenly there seemed nothing to go home for.

The evening dragged, even so. Charlotte didn't get in until eight, but the hours ahead of her seemed like days. There were no distractions at home, there was nothing to stop her from thinking, nothing to stop her

mind going round in circles. And what point was there
in that? No matter how she analysed, no matter how
she raged against Curtis's illogical thinking, there
remained one fact which was unalterable: he didn't
want her enough, he didn't love her.

Later in the week, she bumped into Geoffrey on the
stairs in their building. He immediately started
apologising for his interruption the previous Friday,
and Charlie snapped at him.

'For goodness' sake, Geoffrey, leave it alone! You
made your apology at the time. Honestly, anyone
would think——' She bit the words off, unsure how to
end the sentence.

They had reached her landing, were standing near
her front door. Geoffrey glanced at it, his eyes
troubled as they came back to her. 'May I come in for
a moment?'

'No.' She turned away but he put a restraining hand
on her arm.

'Look, Charlie, I don't know why your boy-friend
walked out like that last week, but I do realise what I
interrupted. I won't deny I'm as jealous as hell. I
disliked Curtis Maxwell on sight. He has everything I
haven't got, sophistication, money, looks and—*you*.
You're in love with him, it's as plain as the nose on
your face. But he's let you down, hasn't he? I saw how
you looked on Monday morning. I had the day off,
drove past you in the opposite direction when you
were walking to the Underground. You must have
been very late for work. You looked like death warmed
up then, and you still do.'

Charlotte's shoulders slumped. Did she really look
so bad, so white-faced? She felt the sting of tears in
her eyes. Geoffrey's little speech was hard to handle,
honest as it was. He was concerned for her, indignant
for her, she could hear it in his voice. She glanced
towards her front door. 'O.K., you're welcome to a
cup of coffee, if you like.'

Geoffrey jumped at the offer.

'It's over between me and Curtis,' she told him as she put two steaming mugs of coffee on the low table in the living-room. 'And I've no wish to talk about it, Geoffrey.'

'It might help.'

It might, but it would alter nothing, and besides, it would hardly be fair to him. He was far too fond of her to be objective. 'I'll tell you how you can help me,' she said suddenly. 'But I'd be using you. I must be honest about that.'

He smiled. 'That's what friends are for. People like to be used from time to time—friends, I mean. It reassures them that they *are* friends, that they're needed. So what can I do for you, lovely lady?'

She smiled, determinedly trying to brighten up. 'You can take me out.'

'Done! Give me an hour to——'

'No, I didn't mean tonight.' She even laughed a little. 'You're very sweet, you know that?'

'Yeah, yeah.' His smile was wry. 'I'm the sweet and dependable guy next door. So when can I take you out?'

'At the weekend.' The weekend. That would be the worst time. She would need all the distraction she could get.

'Well, I've got commitments on Sunday but I'm free on Saturday. Will that do? I mean, will it help?'

'Very much so.'

'And where would you like to go?'

Curtis wouldn't have asked that. He would have told her where they were going. He would have had his own plans. 'Anywhere,' she said ungraciously. 'I mean, well, surprise me.'

Geoffrey managed to do that. He phoned her at the office on Friday, telling her they were going out for the entire day on Saturday, that she had to get a picnic together.

'I'll shop for it tonight,' she told him, looking forward to it not in the least. The shopping or the picnic.

'And in the evening,' Geoffrey went on, sounding pleased with himself, 'we're going to the ballet. I've got the best seats in the place.'

'How on earth did you manage that at such short notice?'

There was a smile in his voice. 'Just a lucky break. I bought them from one of my colleagues. He booked weeks ago but he can't make it. His wife's mother—oh, never mind all that! I've got 'em now. Front stalls. O.K.?'

'O.K.!' This was more like it. It had been a long time since Charlotte had been to the ballet, she would enjoy it. She put the phone down, noticing Linda's look of curiosity. 'That was Geoffrey,' she told her. 'He's taking me out for the day tomorrow. And in the evening we're going to the ballet. You see, Linda, there are plenty more fish in the sea.'

Linda said nothing.

Saturday began well, weather-wise. They drove out to the countryside in Geoffrey's car, the picnic packed in the boot, looking for the perfect spot. They ended up eating in the car. Clouds gathered and quite suddenly the heavens opened. If there was a funny side to the scene, Charlie couldn't see it, though had she been herself she would have. As for her companion, he was positively annoyed. All the time they were eating he went on and on about the weather.

Without the mutual interest of rehearsals, of a new play, between them, she and he had run out of conversation. She was glad he'd been unable to offer her his company for the Sunday, glad she would be inside a theatre with him that night. Basically, she had nothing in common with Geoffrey Hemmings. He didn't even have a sense of humour.

They got home around four, going their separate ways into their flats, agreeing they would leave for the ballet around six-thirty, give themselves time to find a parking place and to have a drink before the show began. Charlotte bathed and then dressed and made up with care, not for Geoffrey's sake but for her own. She thought it would be good for the morale. She was sick of her pale reflection, sick of her white, freckled face. A subtle application of rouge was called for. If only the weather was more reliable, she could have done some sunbathing. It was a lovely thought, some time in the sun would be very welcome right now.

She had some holiday time coming up—the first two weeks of August, to be precise. It was still a couple of weeks away, and she planned to go home to Kendal. The Lake District was very beautiful at the height of summer. It was, she thought with a sudden pang of homesickness, lovely all the year round.

Like the morning, the evening began well enough. The rain had cleared up and she experienced a ripple of excitement when the orchestra began tuning their instruments. The theatre was splendid, all gilt and chandeliers and plush red seats. Charlotte looked around with interest, taking in the décor and scanning the faces of the audience.

And then she saw Curtis.

He was in one of the boxes, off to the right of the stage. He wasn't alone, there were two of them. Two people sharing the box: Curtis and someone very familiar to Charlotte. She didn't have to wonder where she'd seen the woman before. She remembered clearly, only too clearly. Curtis was with Pippa Loxley, Sir Kevin Loxley's niece, the woman who'd said she lived just ten minutes' drive from Curtis's place. Which place, Charlie didn't know. Not that it mattered. Whether she lived in Buckinghamshire, near Curtis's house, or whether she lived in London, within easy reach of his flat.

All Charlie knew and cared about was that she wanted to get up and leave the theatre now. Now!

She felt sick, sick at heart and foolish with it. Dear God, it hadn't taken him long, had it? Hadn't taken him long to find someone new with whom he could amuse himself. And he would certainly be doing that before the night was out. Pippa Loxley had made her interest in him very, very clear.

Charlie was looking at the programme on her lap, seeing nothing but a blur of print. She couldn't leave, she wouldn't do that to Geoffrey when he'd gone to such trouble to entertain her. Nor would she look up again, not as far as the boxes, at any rate. The sight of Curtis with Pippa, the sure knowledge of what would happen between them before the night was out, made her feel ill.

She hardly saw the ballet, she could see nothing but that which was filling her mind, her imagination. Pictures of Curtis and Pippa. Embracing. Kissing. Making love . . .

'. . . a drink, Charlie?'

'What?' Geoffrey was looking at her. She hadn't even registered that the music had stopped, that the curtain had come down. It was the interval. 'Oh! I—no, I'm so comfy here, I'll pass on the drink, thank you.'

Geoffrey looked surprised. 'I'd like one, actually.'

Involuntarily, Charlotte's eyes went straight to the box. It was empty. No, she absolutely could not risk bumping into Curtis in the bar. She would make a complete fool of herself if that happened. Her jealousy would show, there was no doubt of it. Worse, she might burst into tears. 'Fine,' she said brightly. 'You go ahead.'

Geoffrey looked indignant. 'I'm not going without you! I'll settle for an ice cream. Back in a jiff. Will you have one?'

When at last the show was over, she and Geoffrey left the theatre through one of the side exits. To her profound relief their paths did not cross with those of

Curtis and Pippa. Whether Curtis had spotted her, Charlie had no way of knowing. Probably not. Pippa had been holding his attention very firmly tonight.

As it turned out, Charlie slept well that night. But only because she drank a full bottle of wine when she got in. Only because she sat down and sobbed for two hours. She slept the sleep of the exhausted, of the partially anaesthetised.

It wouldn't do. She told her reflection this the following morning. Her head was pounding, her eyes swollen. Letting the water run cold from the tap, she got some cotton wool and soaked it, held the cold, wet pads against her eyes. 'You've got to pull yourself together. Face it, that man is out of your league. He's very different from you, you should have realised this before. He's hard. With him it's off with the old, on with the new.' Only now was she beginning to realise that Curtis enjoyed his status as a bachelor. Oh, he'd meant all he'd said about his commitment to Chris, but he had, in fact, got the best of all worlds, hadn't he?

He did what he saw as his duty by his sister, and he lived the high life as well. Of course he was happy with the status quo! What did they say, why buy a book when you can join a library? He'd told her he adored women, that there had been many in his life. Oh, yes, he had his life very nicely stitched up! If any of his women were fool enough to fall in love with him, to make demands on him, he had the perfect escape route, hadn't he?

He was selfish, he only thought of *self*. She hadn't realised that before, she'd been too blind to see it.

She, too, was grateful now for Geoffrey's interruption on that awful night. Five minutes later it would have been too late. She and Curtis would have been lovers. And she would be feeling ten times worse than she was feeling now, if that were possible. At least he had had the decency not to do that to her, at least he had shown that much respect for her declaration of love. He wasn't so ruthless, so lacking in integrity that he would make love to a woman and then bid her goodbye the same night.

And so it went. Round and round, round and round. Disgusted with her lack of control, Charlotte made herself get dressed, made herself go out to buy the Sunday papers, the gossipy ones. She didn't normally read any and she immersed herself in them, playing a game with herself, reading story after story and then trying to figure out how much truth there was in them.

It was new to her, feeling loneliness like this. As an only child she had never felt lonely, or at least she was used to aloneness. Aloneness? There was a vast difference in being alone and being lonely. Lonely was what she felt now.

At noon her mother rang. Charlie volunteered nothing, forced herself to sound bright and cheerful, her normal self. But when Pauline asked about Curtis, Charlie tempered the truth. She had to, otherwise she would be asked questions she wasn't up to answering. 'Oh, he's fine, Mummy. I haven't seen him for more than a week, but the last time I saw him, he was fine.'

'Is he away?'

'No, he's in London. Actually, I did get a glimpse of him last night, as it happens. He was at the ballet with Pippa Loxley.'

'Pippa Loxley? But—and who were you with?'

'Geoffrey.'

'But . . .'

'But what?' Charlotte spoke calmly, her answer to her mother's next question already forming in her mind.

'But I've been under the impression that things were quite serious between you and Curtis. I mean, every time I've spoken to you, you've been seeing a lot of him.'

'True. But that doesn't mean we can't go out with other people, does it?'

'Well, that depends——' Pauline broke off. Closing her eyes, disliking herself, Charlotte could almost hear the way her mother's mind was working. She was reaching the decision that her daughter and Curtis Maxwell had not been lovers. Well, that was accurate. 'No, I suppose not. Still, I must say I'm surprised. I had a feeling that something might come of—I'm not going to pry, Charlotte. But please remember that if you feel the need to talk to someone, you can talk to me. You know you can.'

Charlotte was biting her lip now. Oh, it was tempting, so tempting! But it would be unsatisfactory, going into such a long story over the telephone. Besides, her mother would be so biased, so concerned if she knew how heartbroken her daughter was, her sympathy would be intolerable at the moment. 'You're reading too much into it, Mummy.' She kept her voice level. 'Now, what about you? And how's Daddy? What have you been doing this week?'

No sooner had she put the phone down than Chris rang. That was almost too much. Charlie was so taken aback, she almost blurted out to Chris what had happened.

'Chris! I didn't—I mean, this is a surprise. I—didn't expect you to ring me so soon.'

Chris didn't comment. She plunged straight in with an urgent, 'What's the matter, Charlotte? What's happened with you and Curtis?'

'Happened? I don't know what you mean.'

There was a silence.

Charlotte bit hard into her cheeks in an effort to meet silence with silence. She didn't want to volunteer anything, anything at all. But Chris outlasted her, forcing her to speak. 'Chris? Are you still there?'

'I'm here,' she said dully. 'I'll ask you again. What's happened between you and Curtis? I've just phoned him. I did that because I knew something was amiss. You see, *he* hadn't phoned *me*. I hadn't heard from him all week, and that's unheard-of. In fact I hadn't spoken to him since the day he left for New York. At first I assumed he was too preoccupied with you—which, I might add, was an assumption that delighted me. But then his silence went on for too long and I got worried. So I've just phoned him and he happened to mention in passing, ha, ha, as casually as anything, that you and he had called it a day!'

You and he. 'That's—right. Nothing lasts for ever, Chris.'

This was met with an explosion, a protest which contained two or three words Charlotte would never have expected to hear from the older girl. 'Charlotte, do not insult my intelligence! I knew I would get nowhere asking him, but I thought I'd get an answer from you. An honest one, I mean. I was with you and Curtis only two weeks ago, remember? I might be blind, but I am neither deaf nor stupid. I don't need twenty-twenty vision to see that you two are in love. So *what's gone wrong?*'

What could Charlotte say? *You?* 'Honestly, Chris, you're as bad as my mother!' she protested. 'I've just spoken to her, and she's looking for intrigue that doesn't exist. Curtis and I—well, it just didn't work out, that's all.' She went on, not rushing but not allowing time for a reply, either. 'Everything's cool. Neither of us wanted to get heavy, we both want to see other people. As a matter of fact, I saw him out with a lovely-looking woman last night. And I was with a man I go out with from time to time.'

At the sound of Chris's, 'Oh,' Charlotte breathed a sigh of relief. She had convinced her.

Or so she thought.

Christine's next words disabused her of that hope.

'In other words, I should mind my own business.'

It was more than Charlotte could do to be offhand; she liked Curtis's sister too much for that. 'No, Chris,' she said gently. 'I didn't mean that, it isn't that at all.'

'I don't believe you,' came the blunt reply. Blunt but resigned. 'I was going to ask you to come and see me. But you won't, will you?'

'Of course I will. Some time——'

'I meant today.'

'Today! Oh, I—can't. I've got too much to do.' God forgive me! Charlotte closed her eyes, hating the lie. But the idea of visiting Chris was out of the question. Not right now. Not for a long time would she be able to do that. Not until such time as she could be sure not to give anything away. What an awful position she was in! She hated lying to Chris, but how could she tell her the truth?

'Look, Chris, I must go. I—I've got the pressure cooker on the stove and I think it's about to blow its top.'

'I'll tell you something, Charlotte.' There was a sigh. 'You're a hopeless liar!' In the face of the younger girl's silence, Chris added, 'Just promise me one thing, if you feel the need to talk, you'll come to me. I can help you.'

When Charlotte hung up, she was crying again. She had thanked Chris for the offer, using all her willpower to keep her voice light. Help her? No, oh, no. 'Dear Chris,' she muttered to herself, 'you're the one person who can't help me!'

CHAPTER TWELVE

'DAMMIT!' It was too much. It had happened once too often. Charlotte grabbed hold of the single-bud vase and flung it furiously into the wastebin. She succeeded in smashing it, as she had intended to. She should have done it before now. Another week had passed. It was Friday evening, two weeks since the day Curtis had broken off with her, since the day she had thrown the red rose away. Oh, what an omen there had been in its dying that day, after all! Every day and every evening since, she had looked at that empty vase. It had mocked her. She should have put it away there and then.

Now she had smashed it. And with such violence! She sat down at the table, her head in her hands. This time the tears came silently, trickling down her cheeks and creeping under her fingers. The passage of time had not helped one iota. She wasn't herself, she would never be the girl she used to be. There was so much emotion locked inside her, she felt she would burst.

The silence of the flat closed in on her. An hour passed and she just sat weeping at the kitchen table. Eventually she pulled herself together, made a cup of tea and gave herself a good mental shake. Next Friday would be her last day at work. After that, she was on holiday for a couple of weeks. What a jolly time she would have then, without work to keep her occupied! What was she going to *do*? Going home to Kendal did not appeal to her in the least, not any more.

She would book a holiday. Tomorrow was Saturday. She would make it her business to go to the travel agent's and book a holiday. Without fail, she would do it, she would take a holiday in the sun. Anywhere would do. Just—just to get *away*.

She had been through the gamut of emotions. Anger, resentment, bitterness, she'd thought of Curtis with all of these. It was no use. She loved him, plainly and simply. Never in her life had she missed anyone the way she missed him. Every time she looked around her living-room, she saw him there in her mind's eye. He was *inside* her mind, *inside* her heart. She couldn't exorcise him. And, oh, his being there hurt. *It hurt.*

Today had been difficult. She had had to talk to Curtis's secretary about the return of his paintings. Next week would be the third and last week of the Licer exhibition, which had been a great success. The paintings were to be returned to Curtis on the Friday afternoon. They were all to go back to the Mayfair gallery, whence they came. Why this was so when their home was in Buckinghamshire, Charlotte didn't know. She just followed his secretary's instructions. And his secretary, in turn, followed his.

Helen Smith had actually volunteered a little information today. She had been with Curtis for several years. Charlotte knew that, so she knew it was safe to mention his house in Buckinghamshire. Helen, obviously, would know about it, would know that was where her boss kept his private collection.

'Wouldn't it be more sensible to send them directly to his home?' Charlotte had asked.

'Oh, Mr Maxwell doesn't keep these with the rest of his collection. They live here, wrapped up and locked away.'

'That—seems a shame.' Charlotte was very puzzled to hear that.

'Doesn't it just?' Helen agreed. 'Anyway, that's the way it is, I've no doubt he has his reasons. Charlotte, I must go. The other line's ringing, and I expect it's him. He's in Amsterdam this week, but he's still managing to keep me busy! 'Bye!'

There had been no opportunity to learn more. Still, what difference did it make? What did it matter whether he was in Amsterdam or on the other side of Jupiter?

And yet . . . and yet it did make a difference. Fool that she was, Charlie still jumped every time her doorbell rang, every time the phone rang. Fool that she was, she lived in hope that Curtis might come back to her.

'That's what love does for you,' she whispered to herself, looking at the now empty window-sill. 'It makes you behave illogically.' She dragged herself to her feet and set about making supper. She was one of the few people she knew who couldn't afford to lose any weight. 'And when you've had something to eat,' she told herself, 'you will go out. To the pictures or something. It doesn't matter. Just get yourself out of this flat.'

Which she did. Friday evening was spent in the cinema, watching some foreign film with sub-titles she didn't bother to read. On Saturday, first thing, she went to the travel agent's and was told there might be a problem fixing her up. A week was very short notice, she was told.

'And the first two weeks of August are peak holiday weeks.'

Charlotte looked at the young man behind the counter, shook her head in disbelief. 'What's the matter with you?' she snapped. 'Don't you want my business?'

His mouth fell open.

She relented at once, shocked at herself. 'I'm sorry. Look, there's only me. Just a couple of weeks for one little person. Surely you can find me something? I don't care where it is, as long as there's some sunshine. If you can't get me into a hotel, there must be an apartment somewhere. I mean, people cancel at the last minute, don't they? Come to think of it, I'd prefer an apartment.'

'I'll do my best.' The young man was suppressing a

smile now. 'I'm sure I can find something for one—er—little person.'

Charlotte drew herself up to her full five feet eight, smiled down at him benignly and gave him her telephone number. She promptly took herself off to the West End and spent the day shopping for some suitable clothes. Yet while she was doing so, she managed to forget that the holiday was not actually arranged yet, and stayed in the West End until six that evening. By the time she got home, it was too late for the travel agent to ring her; they closed at five thirty.

'I'll ring him from work Monday morning.' She was talking to herself again. It had been good for the spirits, though, having a spending spree. She took her new purchases into the bedroom and tried them all on. An hour later she went out again, determined not to mope, determined not to think. The idea of calling on Geoffrey occurred to her but she dismissed it. She might just as well be alone. Geoffrey Hemmings did not have the power to distract her from anything.

The phone woke her at eight the next morning. Charlotte was fast asleep. She looked groggily at the alarm clock she hadn't set and wondered who would be so thoughtless as to ring a person at eight on a Sunday morning. It certainly wouldn't be one of her parents; they knew only too well that she slept late when she had the chance.

It was Christine.

'Chris!' Panicking, Charlotte pushed the tumble of hair from her face, instantly awake and alert. Christine sounded worried 'What's wrong?'

'Nothing—everything. I'm worried, Charlotte. I want to talk to you. I must. I'm sorry to ring you so early, but I tried to reach you Friday night, then all day yesterday and last night—I was beginning to think you'd gone away.'

The lie came more easily this time. 'I've been living it up a little lately. So tell me, what's wrong?'

'It's Curtis. He——'

'Curtis!' Charlotte's heart started pounding with alarm.

'He's in Amsterdam. He phoned me from there Friday evening. He's on a buying expedition.'

Charlotte relaxed, swamped with relief. 'Then he is all right.'

'No, he isn't. That's just the point. Charlotte, I *have* to talk to you, but not over the phone. Please—can you come and see me today? You could be here in a couple of hours, take the train from Paddington and get a taxi from the station here.'

Not knowing what to say, Charlotte said nothing. 'Charlotte? Say something! If that causes problems, I'll come to you,' Chris went on. 'Either way. It makes no difference to me.'

'But—but what do you want to talk about, exactly?' Charlotte was wary, very wary. What had Curtis said to her? She asked, 'What's worrying you, Chris? What did Curtis say when he phoned you?'

'Charlotte, *please!*' Chris's voice rose. There was a catch in it. 'I can't discuss this over the telephone. Please let me come and talk to you!'

'No, I'll come to you.' What choice did she have? The older woman sounded almost frantic! 'Of course I'll come. Give me the address, I'll get the first train out.'

'Oh, thank God! You'll have no problem finding me, just tell the taxi driver you want the Forest Hill Home for the Blind.'

'The Forest Hill Home for the Blind.' Charlotte climbed into the taxi outside Cheltenham Spa railway station. She sat back in the seat, admiring what she could see of the town as the driver threaded his way through it. She'd never been to Cheltenham before, it was a pretty place.

What did Chris want? What was wrong with Curtis?

As the taxi left the town behind it, the beauty of the Cotswolds, as it had on the train, again struck Charlie as being equal to, though different from, that of her own beloved Lake District. She was lucky, really, to feel as much at home in town or country.

She was panicking inwardly. This interlude with Chris was not going to be easy. She would have to be very careful not to give anything away, not to make Chris feel as if she were some sort of burden. The ultimate burden!

Perspiration trickled down the side of her temple. She shoved her heavy mane of hair away impatiently. She'd been craving for sunshine, and now that there was some it was too hot. At least, it was inside the stuffy taxi. To make matters worse the driver was puffing on a pipe, yet in the back of the car was a sign saying No Smoking. That was some system he had!

'Do you want the main entrance?'

They were on a long curving driveway, at the bottom of which was something resembling a stately home. But she had seen the sign at the top of the drive. This was it. 'I suppose so. I've never been here before. Actually, I'm visiting a friend in one of the wings, the Maxwell Wing.'

'Ah, that's the new part. Well, the newer part, I should say. It was built on—what?—about fourteen, fifteen years ago. The entrance to it is round the back. It connects on the inside with the main part of the building.' The taxi driver was pointing.

'It's quite a place, isn't it? I'll bet it was in its heyday, when it was a private house.'

'It's quite a place now, dear. Wait till you get a look inside. I'm up here several times a week, you know. Got my regulars here, same as umpteen other places.'

He delivered Charlie to a door which had brass name-plates on it. 'If you ring the bell you want, you'll hear your friend speak to you. It's one of those systems. Understandable. Got to be security-conscious

these days, haven't you? Especially with these people
here being blind and all.'

Charlie paid him, pushed the bell above Christine's
name and waited.

'Charlotte?'

She spoke into the little grille. 'Yes, it's me, Chris.'
There was a click. The front door opened.

'Come in. I'm on the first floor. Take the stairs on
your right, there are fourteen steps—oh, what am I
saying?' There was a puff of impatience. 'Up the
stairs, look to your right and you'll see me standing in
the hall.'

A few moments later they were face to face. Chris
was standing about half-way down a long hall.
'Charlotte? Ah, yes, I've just caught a whiff of your
perfume. Welcome.'

As Charlotte stepped in to the hallway of Chris's flat
she was greeted by an immaculately groomed
Labrador.

'This is Della, my guide dog.'

'Hello, Della.' Charlotte laughed as she was sniffed
at, investigated. When she was satisfied she'd passed
Della's test, she stooped and petted her, ruffling her
beautiful golden-coloured coat. 'You're gorgeous,
gorgeous!'

'That's enough,' Chris put in. 'It'll go to her head!
Della, scoot! Into your bed, please.'

The dog obediently took herself off.

'Oh, this is lovely!' As Charlie preceded Chris into
the living-room, she looked around in delight. The
halls and stairs had been carpeted lushly in bottle
green. Here in the flat the carpet was of the palest
green, as were the curtains at a vast window. The
windows were in fact sliding doors and were open,
allowing the warm breeze to drift into the room.
Beyond them was a sun-terrace. All the flats on the
upper floors had terraces, Charlie had seen that from
the outside.

The furniture was modern but plush. The walls were off-white, emulsioned, and on one of them was a unit of shelves housing two tape recorders, a radio and a stereo unit. But the biggest wall, the one which faced the window, was empty except—except that there was a mark on it. A mark which was darker than the rest of the paint. A mark, where a painting had been hanging, a large painting. Charlie stared at it, frowning. She knew why the painting was missing; she knew which painting it was.

She made no comment about it. Instead she remarked on Christine's plants. There were eight of them in all, five of which were hanging from baskets. 'They're in such beautiful condition. Honestly, I'm useless with houseplants! I think I kill them with kindness.'

'You mean you drown them,' Chris laughed. She didn't seem at all worried now. 'I suppose it might seem strange to you, my having plants dotted around. I've got them in every room. But I enjoy them even though I can't see them.'

Just as she enjoys the painting of her mother, Charlie thought. 'It doesn't seem strange at all. You can touch them, smell them. You know what they look like. Besides, they put oxygen in the room or something, don't they?'

'Good heavens, that would be my last reason for having them! Sit yourself down, Charlotte. Are you wearing a jacket? No. Right, make yourself comfortable. I'll put the kettle on. I've got a tray set for tea, and I'll make us some sandwiches.'

It was lunchtime, but Charlotte wasn't hungry. Food was the furthest thing from her thoughts. 'I don't want anything to eat, thanks. Can I help you?' She was impressed. Never having known a blind person before, she hadn't realised what they were capable of doing for themselves.

'No, that's O.K. All I would ask of you is that you

keep your handbag off the floor, or somewhere I'm not likely to trip over it—and don't move anything without telling me. Sorry about that! You'll get used to me.'

It wasn't the first time Chris had said that. It wasn't the first time Charlotte wished she would get the chance. Well, the pleasantries were over now. She braced herself. 'You sounded so worried on the phone. What's wrong?'

'Just a minute.' Christine refused to say anything until she'd brought the tea. She placed the tray on a low table in front of the settee, sat down next to Charlotte and told her she could take over and do the pouring. 'You'll get your tea a little bit faster that way. Now, it's about him, that idiot brother of mine.'

Her expression changed totally. Gone was the light-heartedness. She was frowning now, the loveliness of her features losing nothing in the process. 'I have to apologise to you first, Charlotte. I—well, in a way I tricked you into seeing me. I lied, sort of. I'm not worried about Curtis, I'm *furious* with him.'

Tensing, her hands busy with the teacups, Charlie was unable to say anything.

'I've only spoken to him twice since that weekend we were together, when he took off for New York. The last time was on Friday evening. As I told you, he's in Amsterdam—at least he was, he said he was leaving for Germany the next day. He *says* he's on a buying trip.'

'But—why should you doubt it?' Charlie had no idea where this was leading. 'Surely there's nothing unusual in that?'

'Nothing at all. Except that he has expert staff who normally go buying for him. These days he doesn't go abroad all that much, unless there's something very special he's after. And except that he went on to tell me he'd be moving on to France when he's finished his business. Except that he's going to stay there for "several weeks". Except that he "needs" a long holiday, all of a sudden!' Chris broke off, clicking her tongue in annoyance. 'I've never known him take a holiday for more than two weeks. He's easily bored, you know. I've never known him stay away from his business for—what will it amount to? A couple of months! And get this, he told me he's staying in a villa in the South of France, a place owned by a friend of his. That's fair enough in itself, but he went on to say that I shouldn't worry if I don't hear from him for some time, that the nicest thing about this villa is that it doesn't have a telephone!'

For a moment, Charlotte wondered if she'd been wrong about Chris. Was she feeling insecure now? Worried by the prospect of her brother's absence, his silence?

No sooner had she thought this than she was disabused. Forcefully. 'It was like talking to a brick wall, Charlotte! I couldn't get one straight answer from him. I asked him what he thought he was doing, hiding himself away. And do you know what he said? He said he needed a rest! Did you ever hear anything like it?'

Silence.

'I see.' Christine's smile was wry. 'So that's how it is. A conspiracy, eh? You disappoint me, Charlotte. You've dropped that teaspoon twice and if you don't stop stirring your tea, you'll grind a hole in the bottom of the cup. You're as taut as the strings on a violin. Your vibes are almost prickling me!'

Charlie stopped what she was doing instantly. How was she going to get through this? Like Curtis, Christine didn't miss a thing. She had a mind like a rapier and, like her brother, she had her own way of knowing how Charlie was feeling. Moreover, she knew precisely what was going on. In fact, she knew more than Charlotte herself.

'He's in love with you, Charlotte.'

'No.' The word came dully, adamantly.

With a sound of disgust, Chris got to her feet. She moved around impatiently, finally leaning an elbow on a shelf, turning to the younger girl. 'We're going to get nowhere, nowhere, if you carry on like this. Charlotte, I'm not going to say this is none of my business. It *is*. I'm involved. I don't know what Curtis told you, what he didn't tell you. But you're not leaving this flat until I find out. Now, answer me this. Who finished with whom?'

It was no use. There was no point in trying to evade this woman. She was too wise, too sharp, far too intelligent to be treated as though she were a child. With a long sigh, Charlie said, 'He finished with me.'

'Ah, now we're getting somewhere. Now, at least, you'll admit you're in love with him.'

'Helplessly. Hopelessly.'

Chris nodded. 'And you were daft enough to let him go?'

'Daft enough?' Charlie was annoyed at that. 'Do you think I had a choice? He doesn't—and this really doesn't involve you at all, believe me—Curtis does not love me. It's as simple as that.'

'Rubbish!'

Charlie blinked. She had not expected such directness. Chris was certainly full of surprises! Had Charlotte not been so tense and nervous, she'd have laughed it off. As it was, she burst into tears.

Chris was at her side in a flash. She took her in her arms and held her close, encouraging the tears. 'Go on, love, let it out. Oh, what an awful time you've had this past couple of weeks! You've had your own taste of hell, haven't you?' She murmured on, not expecting an answer. 'Oh, I could throttle Curtis for this! That damn fool darling brother of mine, and this is all because of me. I could *throttle* him.'

Suddenly Charlotte was laughing and crying at the

same time. She was laughing at Christine's vehemence, sagging against her with relief, the relief of being able to talk, at least to some extent. And she was crying because of the sheer kindness, as well as her other reasons. She didn't want to say anything more until she was calm. It was important to wait until she was thinking more clearly, she still had to be careful what she said.

And the question came, inevitably. 'What reason did he give for breaking off with you?'

'He—I think he assumed I would want him to marry me. I—you see, I was stupid enough to tell him I love him.'

'What did he say? How did he react?'

Silence.

'I'm sorry,' Charlie said at length. 'We ... the circumstances were ... I'm blushing, Chris. Would you believe it? We were in the throes—we were about to go to bed.'

'I'm sorry,' Chris groaned. 'I don't want to pry, but—well, it's so important, I have to. I have to know how his mind is working.'

'It's all right.' What the hell? Christine surely knew her brother was no virgin! 'It would have been for the first time. And for me it would have been the—the first time ever. I was stupid enough, or wise enough, to tell him that, too.' She went on, less hesitantly, to tell her about Geoffrey's interruption, of the way Curtis had stalked out of her flat and come back at one in the morning.

'And?'

Charlie closed her eyes. Looking into the intense blue of Christine's was too much like looking into her brother's eyes. 'And then he told me he'd come to say goodbye. Oh, by then I'd realised it was coming. To be fair, he told me right at the start that he'd never marry.'

'He *what*?'

Oh, God! Charlotte flinched from the vehemence now. It was out, she'd said it.

'And he told you it was because of me, didn't he?' It wasn't really a question, it was a statement. *'Didn't he?'*

'Yes.' That was a whisper.

'He told you about my accident, that he feels it was his fault.'

'Yes.'

'Dammit!' Chris was on her feet again. It was a long time before she settled down again this time.

Charlotte sat immobile, hating herself. Curtis would hate her for this. Oh, she would never see him again, but what he thought of her mattered very much to her. She couldn't bear the thought of his hating her. What they'd had together had been so—so right, so good. While it lasted. She wanted to keep the memory of that, unsullied, unspoiled for either of them. 'But it isn't only that. There's more to it than his concern for you, Chris. You've got to believe that. I asked him point blank whether he loved me. I was sure we could work something out, that it would work itself out, perhaps. But he said no. He looked me straight in the eye and told me his feelings for me didn't go that far. So your part in this becomes irrelevant.'

'He was lying.' The words were said dismissively. The next ones were said scornfully. 'And now he's gone away! He obviously thinks that if he spends enough time in new surroundings, he'll get over you. The idiot! Surely he realises it's different this time? If I know it, why doesn't he? I can't understand it. It's very, very different!'

Charlie's voice was barely audible. 'This time? What—what do you mean, *this time?*'

CHAPTER THIRTEEN

'I MEAN Curtis was once engaged to be married.' Tiredly, Chris lowered herself into a chair. 'He was only eighteen. That's half a lifetime. His lifetime, at any rate. Our lifetime. No, I tell a lie, this was Christmas and he'd turned nineteen in the November. Anyhow, it wasn't real. He was very young and he merely thought himself in love. But neither of us knew that at the time. He's never mentioned this to you?'

'No.'

'Maybe he's forgotten the girl.'

'You never forget your first love.'

'That's true.' There was a smile, a real smile at last. 'I haven't forgotten mine. I was six at the time. Anyway,' Chris went on, sighing, 'Curtis had spent one term at Cambridge, that's where he'd met the girl—Julie Stevenson. He came home, alone, for the Christmas holidays. We lived in the house in Bucks. Since you know about the accident, you know about the house, I take it?'

'Yes. The accident happened nearby.'

'In the grounds—there are acres of them. Well, to cut a long story short, Curtis announced his engagement as soon as he got home that Christmas. *Fait accompli*. It was unofficial as yet, of course. Well, he was on cloud nine! I'd never met Julie, but I was delighted, for him. Delighted because he was so happy. You see, he'd never known a happy day since I lost my sight. Eight, nine years and he'd never stopped blaming himself. He still hasn't, as you realise only too well. But at the time, thanks to Julie Stevenson, I thought he'd finally managed to put it behind him.

'And then the Maxwells had their second tragedy. My mother died suddenly, on the night before Christmas Eve. It was a brain tumour. Nobody knew anything about it.'

'Oh, Chris! How awful!'

'It gets worse. My parents were young. They were both forty-one. My father was devoted to Mummy, absolutely potty about her. Her death killed him. He never even made it to her funeral. He collapsed with a stroke on Christmas Day. It was so severe, and I have to say I'm thankful for this, it killed him outright. Had he survived it, he would have been paralysed. That would have been too awful to bear, for all of us. He was an extremely clever and active man, a barrister who loved his work almost as much as he loved his family.'

Charlotte was muttering, hardly knowing what to say. To think that in the space of two days, Curtis and Chris had lost both their parents. At the age of forty-one!

'You can imagine,' Chris went on, 'how devastated we were. Quite suddenly we found ourselves alone in the world, sort of thing, and living in that vast house. To be brief, when the emotional fog finally lifted, I took action. Curtis had refused to go back to university. He also said he was going to break off his engagement with Julie. I knew instantly what he was doing. He was thinking of me, he was wondering how I'd cope without my parents. Especially my mother. He was sacrificing himself for me, saying we would carry on in the house together.

'I was appalled, by all of it. We fought like cat and dog. He told me that something had changed inside him, which was feasible, though I didn't believe it. He said he'd realised he wasn't in love with Julie, after all. You can imagine what I said to that!

'As it turned out, it was the truth. But as I say, neither of us knew it right then.

'So, unbeknown to him, with the help of my trustees I made arrangements to come and live here. And I presented *that* as a *fait accompli* to Curtis. When it was all arranged, I announced to him what I was going to do. It had never occurred to him I could live elsewhere, get some training and even find some employment to keep me busy. He went mad, he argued with me night and day. I was immovable, and—well, here I am!'

These were the bare facts, Charlotte realised. She didn't need more. After the death of his parents, eighteen years ago, Curtis had made up his mind he would never marry because he was the only close relative Chris had left in the world. 'He went back to Cambridge, didn't he? He mentioned——'

'Oh, yes. When he saw I wasn't going to change my mind. I freed him—or I thought I did. I also freed myself. I have a good life here, it was the best thing I could have done, finding this place.'

'And the addition of the Maxwell Wing? Was that prompted by Curtis's feelings of guilt?'

'Actually, no. He gives money away like a man with six arms, to all sorts of charities and causes. But that's in his nature, it always was. He was generous from the time he could hand out toffees. Why don't we have some more tea, Charlotte? Or would you prefer coffee?'

'Allow me. Please, I feel the need to move around a bit.'

Chris laughed. 'I know the feeling. Go ahead.'

Charlie did so, taking care to replace everything precisely where she found it. 'I've put the tea-tray on the left-hand draining board, Chris.' She came back to the living-room with two mugs of coffee, placed Chris's on the table at the side of her chair. 'Here we are.'

'Thanks. You know, it's utterly ridiculous keeping that house on. But it was a compromise I made with

Curtis at the time. He refused to sell it in case I wanted to go back at some point. I ask you! Try getting him to change his mind! He's just as bad as I am. To this day he insists on keeping it on, and I rarely go there. Lovely though it is, it's—it's like some kind of shrine to days that have long gone. Not to mention the expense. Do you know how many gardeners he pays just to keep the grounds respectable? Four! Isn't it ludicrous? Fine, if the place were lived in, appreciated. It's a gorgeous house, it should be filled with the sound of laughter, filled with children——' Chris broke off, her eyes uncannily meeting directly with Charlotte's. 'Which brings us back to our problem. What are we going to do?'

'Do? We can't "do" anything.'

'Like hell!'

'Chris, *listen to me*.' Charlotte paused, wondering how to say what she wanted to say. 'Speaking of things ridiculous, I can hardly believe I'm having this conversation with you. For heaven's sake, you're Curtis's *sister*!'

'And the cause of all your problems. Yours and his.'

'*No*, that's just it. You say he loves me, but you're wrong.'

'Charlotte—oh, I know it doesn't look very hopeful, but I know what I'm talking about. I know Curtis inside out. He's battling with himself right now, the poor darling. Torn between his guilt towards me and his love for you. I know I'm right. Nothing will convince me to the contrary.' Chris leaned forward, her long, elegant fingers splayed out. 'The first time he mentioned you to me was the day he met you. He's always told me what he's been doing with his time. I could scream at times! But he means well, it's his way of sharing his life with me. Yet another of his ways. Where was I? Oh, yes, the first time he mentioned you was to say he'd met "a stunner". He told me he'd caught you nattering in the office with that temp he had working for him, when Helen was ill.

'Then I got a bulletin about his taking you to lunch. By that time you'd become fascinating, a really interesting person. I'd never heard him go on so, not with such enthusiasm. To put it simply, it wasn't like him. I was delighted.

'Suffice it to say that as time moved on you changed from being a stunner to being beautiful.' She grinned. 'I'm sure you are, but what's that they say about the eyes of the beholder? Do you catch my drift? And then there was the last night of your play, the day I met you. Curtis collected me from here that morning. If he told me once during the journey, he told me six times he'd be glad when the play was over, so he could see more of you, see you in the evenings. He'd already planned ahead.

'No sooner had we got to his flat than he tried to ring you. It was lunchtime. He thought it would be nice if you joined us. Well, I know he'd been in Brighton for two days. He couldn't wait to see you, didn't want to wait till the evening. Do I have to go on?'

There was a muffled noise from across the room. Charlotte was crying again. That was the day Curtis had given her the rose. He did love her! He knew full well what that flower meant, he hadn't chosen a red rose by chance. Oh, God! She hadn't been mistaken at the time of the preview, when he'd looked at her through eyes filled with love. 'Th-there's only one problem,' she stammered. 'No, I'm all right, really I am. Don't get up.' Charlie fished in her bag for a hanky, blew her nose noisily.

Chris stayed where she was, her heart going out to the younger woman. 'I know,' she said softly. 'And believe me, I intend to have a long talk with that brother of mine.'

'*No!*' Charlotte almost leapt from the settee. '*Think* about it. That's absolutely the wrong thing to do! All right, maybe Curtis does love me. But he doesn't love

me enough. *Enough*, Chris. Enough to think in terms
of permanence. And for me, at this stage . . . well,
nothing else will do. It has to be——' She finished the
sentence to herself. All or nothing. Curtis had used
those words. He'd said it would have to be that way,
with her. And what had he done then? He'd said
goodbye. 'It's up to him,' she went on. 'It has to be.
Leave him be. Let him fight his battle. If he chooses
me, it has to be fair and square, because he really
wants to. I wouldn't have it any other way. You
mustn't try to talk him into anything. You're a
woman, you must understand what I mean. His love,
his need of me has to be stronger than his feelings of
love and guilt towards you. Not in any way must you
try to influence him.'

'Yes,' Chris said softly, 'you're right, absolutely
right. Of course you are. I was only trying——'

'To help. I know that. Well,' added Charlotte,
sniffing, 'you have—a lot. I'll tell you this much, I'd
love to have you as a sister-in-law. You're a wonder, I
think you're marvellous. But you must promise me,
promise me faithfully, that you'll say nothing to
Curtis. Just leave him be.'

The promise was forthcoming. 'I swear. I swear I
won't say a word to him.' Chris's eyes closed
momentarily. She would stand by her word.
Fortunately, however, she had already said to Curtis
what she wanted to say to him now. She'd said it
pertaining to a different woman, different girl.
Eighteen years ago. She only hoped he would
remember.

'Chris?'

'Sorry. I was back in the past for a moment.'

'That's what I wanted to ask you. About the past.
That painting. I mean the painting which lives on
your wall. It's *The Lady in White*, isn't it? Your
mother.'

'Yes. Seeing her in the portrait was almost the last

time I saw my mother. It was the last work of art I was to see. Fernando Licer was staying with us at the time of my accident. He painted the series, the six paintings Curtis put in your exhibition with *The Lady in White*. He did that portrait of Mummy, too, during his stay. Nobody had been allowed a glimpse until it was finished. It was unveiled on the day of the accident, that same morning. We were all present for the unveiling. I thought it was the most beautiful thing I'd ever seen. But my mother was beautiful, Charlotte, she really was. It—the painting means a great deal to me. I don't have to be able to see it to see it.'

At last, at last Charlie understood! Or did she? There was more, she knew it, she just knew it. She was thinking about that certain quality in the painting. She could see the portrait now, in her mind's eye. 'There's more, isn't there? Something you haven't told me?'

'Yes.' Chris was smiling. 'But some of it would be speculation and—well, that's another story.'

Charlie let it rest at that. It was another story. And she would probably never get to hear it. As far as the other six paintings were concerned, the series, she had been very slow; until now she hadn't realised it was the Maxwells' house and grounds they depicted. 'I'd better go now, it's getting late. I've got some ironing to do, got to get my clothes ready for work.'

The phone rang.

Chris reached for it. 'Chris Maxwell.' Her voice changed. The briskness vanished. 'Oh, hello, James. Of course I'm expecting you. Around eight, we said. Yes, I can manage seven, if you'd prefer . . . Fine. No, no, I'm not trying to get rid of you. I have a guest. We were just saying goodbye.'

Were they?

Chris put the phone down. 'That was my latest.'

'Your latest?'

'Lover.' She shrugged. 'Not that there have been

many. I wouldn't like you to get the wrong impression!'

'I—oh!' Her latest lover? What next? 'Is he—I mean——'

'You mean is he blind.' Chris was laughing at her. 'The answer is no. He's the newscaster at the local radio station. I met him a few weeks ago, when I was giving a talk. They tell me he's quite a dish.'

'So are you,' smiled Charlotte.

'So I believe!'

'Does Curtis—I mean, does Curtis know about this?'

'Certainly not. I may or may not mention James in my own good time. I lead my own life, Charlotte.' Chris laughed again, a trifle apologetically, a trifle impishly. 'Sorry. What I mean is, I'll wait and see what happens. Sorry again! But you'll get used to me.'

Oh, Charlie hoped so! She hoped so very, very, much!

CHAPTER FOURTEEN

'THE bad news is that I'll have to pay a hefty supplement because it's an apartment for four. It's got two bedrooms.' Charlotte was relating to her secretary what the travel agent had just said to her.

It was Tuesday. She had given him her work number the previous day and had been offered three different holiday locations. Opting for this one, in an apartment in southern Spain, she'd left him to make the necessary confirmation. He'd only just phoned her back with the final details.

'But you've accepted,' Linda remarked. 'So what was the good news?'

'That this is one of the more prestigious complexes and that I'll be flying from Heathrow rather than Gatwick. It's much more convenient for me.'

'And where is this apartment, exactly?'

'Fuen—Fuengi——' Laughing, Charlie spelt it out.

'Fuengirola.' Linda spoke with authority. 'It's not far from Marbella. Smack in the middle of the south coast, you should get your fair share of sunshine there. Don't you speak any Spanish?'

'*Si, si!*'

'Is that it?'

'*Si!*'

Linda went off into gales of laughter. Oh, it was good to see Charlotte looking more human, being more cheerful. 'Well, I think you'd better learn another word—*no!* Do you think you can remember that? You know what they say about hot-blooded Spaniards!' She calmed down, her eyes questioning. 'But seriously, you might meet someone. Someone who——'

The smile faded from Charlotte's face. Someone who'd take her mind off Curtis? Maybe even replace him? Never! 'Forget it, Linda. Besides, I'm doing just fine as I am.'

Linda did not go on.

It was and it wasn't true. Charlotte was functioning, going about her business with apparent normality. She even laughed from time to time. But inwardly . . . inwardly, it was all crushing her. All the emotion, all the worry, all the wishing and praying and hoping . . .

She snapped out of it, bringing herself back to the matter in hand. 'I'd better go in and see Mr Grant. The travel agent wants my cheque straight away so I'll have to leave early tonight because they close at five-thirty.'

Edward Grant greeted his assiatant as if he hadn't seen her for days. 'Good morning, Charlotte! Come in, come in.'

Sitting, she looked at him a little suspiciously. What was with him?

'The baby,' he announced, 'kicked for the first time yesterday! I told Janice she should have phoned me and let me know. I didn't learn of this till last night.'

He looked thoroughly disgruntled, provoking a smile from Charlie. He was such a sweet man—and he was more or less normal again these days. Apart from these occasional newsflashes about Janice and the baby, he was virtually himself. Except that he was even happier. His happiness was a pleasure to see and it was—enviable. Enviable!

'Well, that is exciting!' She couldn't, wouldn't, let news of this magnitude go unacknowledged. 'And Janice is well?'

'Glowing! Positively glowing! She's coming into town today. I'm taking her out to lunch, so you'll be able to say hello.'

'I'll look forward to it. Um—I came to ask you . . .'

Putting him in the picture about her last-minute holiday arrangements, she got down to business.

'But of course. Leave when you like, Charlotte. Heaven knows you put enough extra hours in these days.' This was accompanied by a searching look. When there was no response, he asked her more about the forthcoming holiday.

They chatted for five or six minutes before getting on with their work. There were no personal questions, though. If Edward Grant knew anything at all about his assistant and Curtis Maxwell, he didn't let Charlotte know it.

'Yes, I've written it down. I can't think of any reason why I should need to get in touch with you. Nobody's ill or anything. Still, I'm happier knowing where you are.'

'Of course.' Charlotte was talking to her mother. It was eight o'clock on the Friday evening, the night before she was to fly to Spain. And she still had so much to do! There was a pile of ironing, buttons to be sewn on, and the keys to her suitcase were nowhere to be found.

'I'd better go, Mummy, I've got lots to do.'

'I can imagine. But—oh, darling, I hate to think of you taking a holiday alone.'

They'd already been through all this. Try as she might, Charlotte had been unable to convince her parents that this was what she wanted. Well, it was and it wasn't. She wanted to get away from all familiar surroundings, but—but on the other hand, she knew she'd be left with too much time to think. Still, the holiday was organised now. It was too late to change her mind. She wouldn't get a refund at this stage. At least she was doing something *positive*, at least she'd made a decision. That was a good sign, wasn't it?

'Now don't fuss. I shall have a good rest. I've already explained why I didn't ask a girl friend to go

with me.' The idea of asking one of her friends from
the drama society had occurred to Charlotte, but she
had dismissed it at once. Two girls on holiday
together, one of them deeply in love and too tender
even to think of going out with another man, the other
probably thinking of nothing but. Dating. And discos
and dancing and . . . no. It wouldn't have worked.

'I didn't believe that, either,' Pauline remarked.

The words, the obvious disappointment with which
they were spoken, made Charlotte feel ashamed. She
had never come clean with her mother, had evaded any
questions about Curtis. It was wrong of her. Only now
did she realise it. Her relationship with her mother had
always been an honest one; they had always been good
friends, even when Charlotte was a teenager. She
sighed, apologising now. 'I'm sorry, Mummy. I—it's
true that I need a rest. I've worked hard all year.
But—well, I don't want company. That's the top and
bottom of it. Not even yours and Daddy's. The truth is,
as I'm sure you already know, I'm not over Curtis yet. I
didn't want to finish it, he did.'

'But why?'

'He's—simply not the marrying kind.' Enough was
enough. There was no way she could begin to explain
further over the phone. Besides, it was irrelevant now.
Curtis had removed himself from her life and he
wasn't coming back. Had there been any hope of that,
he would have turned up by now.

At ten that evening she was still ironing. The keys
to the suitcase had been found. Everything was in
hand. When the doorbell rang, Charlie let out a sound
of impatience. She wasn't expecting anyone. Geoffrey
had already said his goodbyes and that he was going
out for the evening.

Evidently he had not. He was standing on her
doorstep. 'Hi! Just thought I'd see if I could help you
in any way. Do you need a suitcase sitting on or
something?'

'Come in, you idiot! I'm not taking that much with me!' She went straight back to the ironing-board, leaving him to trail after her.

'Good grief. Then why are you ironing that lot?'

'I'm only taking——' She broke off abruptly. The bare essentials, she'd been about to say. Remembering the day Curtis had collected her, when he drove her to Kendal for the weekend. He'd teased her about how much she'd packed for a couple of days. That was the trouble, one of the many difficulties she was living with now. She was always remembering ... kisses, conversations, the touch of his hand on hers, the uncanny way he had of knowing what she was feeling, the way he'd teased her that time about being Charlotte the harlot, the way he'd looked when ... 'Why aren't you out with the boys?' she said instead.

Geoffrey had flopped into an armchair, looking very sorry for himself. 'I was supposed to be out with a girl, actually.'

'And?'

'And she stood me up. The fool! She doesn't know what she's missing.'

Charlie smiled obligingly. 'Make yourself useful, then! Get me a cup of coffee, would you?'

It was seven in the morning when Charlotte next had a cup of coffee. She switched everything off before leaving her flat, put her passport in her handbag and took one last look around.

She got to Heathrow in plenty of time; she'd had to get there even earlier than the requisite pre-flight time because of the tickets. They were here at the airport. Or so she hoped. She'd allowed herself an extra half-hour in case of hitches, in case frantic phone calls had to be made or computers took sick or something.

There were no hitches. Moreover, the flight to Malaga was as smooth as one could hope for. On the other hand, it wasn't exactly uneventful. She was on an Iberian Airways Airbus and she had, unfortunately, been given a seat in a row of two, by the window. The man who was sitting next to her talked incessantly, even when she closed her eyes and tried to feign sleep! Charlie privately gave him one out of ten for his chatting-up technique, relegating him under the heading of boring in spite of his good looks. He was around thirty, he was travelling alone and, thank goodness, was staying nowhere near Fuengirola. If she refused one drink from him, she refused five.

It was only when she was waiting for her luggage by the carousel in Malaga airport that she supposed she should be flattered. The man was standing just a few yards from her now, having given up completely. And he was good-looking, very. She shrugged mentally; he was no doubt aware there were plenty more fish in the sea.

Why couldn't she think in these terms?

'Taxi?'

'Taxi?'

There was a chorus of voices, a small sea of faces as she emerged through customs, into the main concourse of the airport. Taxi drivers in a cluster, competing with sheer enthusiasm for custom. Charlie picked a face she thought she could trust and told him to take her to the Apartamentos Villa Rosa, in Fuengirola.

From then on, her luggage was carried for her. She settled in the back of the taxi and, finally, relaxed. This week had been a busy one, dashing to the bank in quest of *pesetas*, leaving everything in order at work. Delegating to Linda. Washing, ironing, and all.

Her spirits lifted considerably. The sun was shining. And how! It was positively scorching, not a cloud in sight. There was silence, too, quite a change after what she'd been subjected to on the plane. This taxi driver was clearly not the chatty type, and had he been, he'd have got precisely nowhere! Yes and no were literally all Charlie knew of the Spanish language. She spoke

French fluently, but that would hardly do her much good here!

She concentrated on the passing scenery, refusing to let her mind wander just because she had happened to think about French. France. South of.

On her right were the Sierra Blanca mountains, on her left the magnificent blue of the Mediterranean. They passed through several towns, separated by long stretches of open countryside, beachside, as yet undeveloped areas. There was, she thought wryly, plenty more room for hotels. She wondered what this coast must have been like thirty, twenty years ago. Little fishing villages, no doubt. Picturesque. Uninvaded by the sun-seekers. But nothing stayed the same, did it?

The Apartamentos Villa Rosa came into sight a little under an hour after leaving the airport. Charlie's spirits lifted even more. The apartments were built in three blocks, in a U-shape. In the centre of them was a swimming-pool, twinkling blue under the sun. Around the poolside were an occasional tree giving shade, sunbeds and small tables. Plants were growing everywhere, their colours brilliant in purples, blues, oranges and yellows. There was an outside bar, covered by a red-and-white striped canopy, and she saw a sign pointing to the restaurant which was on the ground floor in the centre block. Yes, this would do nicely!

Charlotte paid the taxi driver, tipped him so that he beamed with gratitude, and let the concierge take care of her luggage. She walked after him towards a flight of stairs, noting that he ignored the lift. Therefore, she was probably on the first floor.

She was. The apartment itself was super, its windows shuttered against the sun, its walls stark white to give the illusion of coolness. The furniture was typically Spanish, the floor tiled and covered partly by rugs. Charlie choose the bedroom which did

not overlook the swimming-pool, unpacked her bags
and went into the compact kitchen to make herself
some coffee. Except that there wasn't any. Of course
there wasn't.

She went out, certain that where there were
apartments such as these, there would be a super-
market not too far away.

It was on her third day that she got round to writing
postcards, hoping they would reach England before
she did. She really had no idea how long post took to
travel from Spain. To Linda she wrote a jocular:
'This place is here! Wish you were lovely.' Linda
would giggle at that.

By her fifth day she was bored rigid. She had eaten
in the restaurant each evening, simply because it was
too awful sitting in the apartment and eating alone. Of
course, she had been asked out, by some married
couples as well as three or four—or was it five?—single
men who were staying there. People she'd chatted to
around the pool.

It was on her eighth day that there was a telephone
call for her. By then she was thoroughly fed up and
wishing herself back at work. And she had made an
effort, she'd gone out with one of the married couples,
who were really very nice people, and she'd eaten out
alone in one of the local restaurants, for a change.

'Señorita? Telefono!'

Charlotte was stretched out on a sunbed by the
pool. Only once had she spent the day on the beach.
She preferred the grounds here because she was
happier swimming in a pool than in the sea. She
peered through her sunglasses at the young man, the
uniformed teenager who was one of the staff.

Surely he was mistaken? 'Telephone? For me? Are
you sure it's for me?'

The boy was nodding vigorously. 'Si, si, para
Señorita Car-lote Gra-am.'

It was a fair approximation of her name. There was

no mistake. Suddenly she was on her feet, grabbing her wrap and tying it hastily around her. Something had to be wrong, terribly wrong! She had given the address and telephone number of the apartment only to her mother.

Her *mother*! Oh, God. Not her parents! Surely something couldn't have happened to one of her parents?

Following the young porter, she dashed into the shade of the building and snatched up the phone in the booth which was pointed out to her.

The line was dead.

She spun round, calling to the telephone operator behind the desk. 'The line's dead!'

'*Señorita?*'

'I—there's nobody here. No phone call!'

'*Si*, it was a lady. She ask for you.'

Five minutes later Charlotte went back to her sunbed. The line had been dead. The operator had switched switches to no avail. His English was reasonable and he'd explained that this happened sometimes. He'd said the same thing when Charlotte tried to return her mother's call. This happens sometimes. The international lines are all engaged. Just wait a while and try again.

She would. And she wouldn't rest until she got through.

Fishing in her bag for her watch, Charlie shaded her eyes against the sun. It was eleven-thirty. What day was it? Sunday. She lay back, closing her eyes and worrying. Why would her mother ring her here at eleven-thirty on a Sunday? Why should she ring her at all? Something awful had happened. It must have.

Ten minutes later she decided to try again. She was just putting her watch back in her bag when she spotted him. When her heart stopped.

Rendered immobile, her lips parted in disbelief, Charlotte stared as Curtis walked towards her. It was only when the shadow of his body was covering her that she knew he was real, not a product of imagination, of wishful thinking.

'Hello, Charlotte.' He wasn't smiling, he was probing her eyes with his own, worriedly, searchingly. 'I've been a complete and utter fool,' he said simply. 'Can we talk?'

CHAPTER FIFTEEN

They walked into the cool of the apartment building, saying nothing for the moment. Charlotte hadn't said a word, not even as much as hello, she had been too stunned. Her legs felt as though they were about to give way beneath her. In her mind there were a dozen questions, milling around in confusion.

'*Señorita!*' the switchboard operator called to her just as they were approaching the stairs. 'One moment, please. The English lady is on the line again.'

'Excuse me.' She left Curtis, headed for the booths where the phones were. She was no longer panicking, not about her parents, at any rate. By now she'd guessed what had happened. 'Hello. Is it you, Mummy?'

'Charlotte? Oh, thank goodness!' Her mother's voice was tight with anxiety. 'I tried to reach you last night but you were out. Are you all right?'

'Yes. I——'

'Good. Listen, I'm ringing to warn you you might get a phone call from Curtis. I've been trying to reach you since nine this morning, but getting through was difficult. You see, he phoned me from France last night and demanded to know where you were. I assumed I was doing the right thing in giving him—— '

'He's here, Mummy. He arrived about five minutes ago.'

'He's *there*? In person?'

Charlotte smiled without humour. 'In person.'

'Oh! I wonder how he managed that? I—well, I'll go, then. I can't imagine . . . oh, never mind. What I really want to say is good luck, darling.'

Charlie replaced the receiver gently, thoughtful. Oh, Mum! How right you were! You once said that the ways of the world seemed so simple to me, so black and white. How naïve I was then, how lacking in . . . but not any more! I've learned a great deal in a short time.

Curtis was waiting by the stairs. 'It was my mother,' she said, hardly able to look at him. Her heart was pounding like a mad thing. Hope and fear were battling for precedence inside her. 'She phoned to warn me you might ring me today.'

He acknowledged with a nod, a mirthless smile. 'I was trying to ring you at your flat all day yesterday. I had no idea about this holiday. Eventually I phoned your parents, I assumed you'd gone home for the weekend.'

It was only when they got in to her apartment that she took a proper look at him. He was tanned, tense, his shirt darkened with patches of perspiration. It was startling to see him looking less than immaculate, dressed in denim, his shoes covered in dust.

'How—how did you get here, Curtis? You look as if you've walked.' Charlotte was standing in the middle of the room, looking just as awkward as she felt. Curtis was a few feet away from her, his own stance telling of the tension inside him. The very air was crackling with it.

'I got a lift down from France. I've been staying in the South of France, in a villa with an old friend. He has his own plane. I asked him to bring me down here. There was no way I could get a seat on a commercial flight. I—suppose it's the time of year and all that.'

'I suppose. Well, that was—handy.'

'I know several people who're mad about flying, who have their own aircraft.' And then he grinned. 'I have friends in high places.'

The tension broke. Charlotte laughed in spite of herself. Curtis took two strides and enfolded her in his arms, his hands sliding into her hair as he held her tightly against him. 'Oh, Charlotte, Charlotte . . .'

She closed her eyes, still unable to believe what was happening, that he was here. She clung to him, revelling in the security of being in his arms. Friends in high places? Well, so had she. She said a silent prayer of thanks.

'Let me get you something to drink.' She moved away from him reluctantly. 'You must be parched. Would you like something cold? I've got some lager in the fridge.'

'Lovely. Is there somewhere I can wash?'

Charlotte pointed the way to the bathroom. In the kitchen she poured two glasses of lager, put them on a tray with two unopened cans. Calmness had descended over her. It was going to be all right. Then she thought about Chris and she leaned on the sink with both arms, steadying herself because all calm and control suddenly vanished. Please, please, she prayed, don't let me discover that Chris is responsible for his being here. If he had also phoned Chris yesterday, if he had phoned her *first*, if she had told him . . .

'Darling? Here, let me take that.' Curtis took the tray into the living-room, eased himself tiredly into an armchair. He polished off his lager thirstily, refilling his glass from another can. 'Thanks. I needed that.'

Their eyes met and held. 'Charlotte, oh, Charlotte, can you forgive me? I know what I've put you through.'

'I can forgive you anything.' Her voice, steady as it was, belied what was going on inside her. 'Why are you here, Curtis? What do you want to say?'

'That I love you,' he said simply. 'That I can't live without you.' His smile was self-mocking. 'Of course I can live without you. But let me put it this way: I don't want to. I want you. I want you to be my wife, the mother of my children, my companion, my friend, my lover. I want you to make my life whole, to make me whole. I need you, I——' He stopped, unable to go on.

Charlotte had heard the catch in his voice. She was nodding, her head moving slowly up and down in understanding, her eyes closed now. His proposal, she thought, had been beautiful. When she opened her eyes, there were tears in them. Letting out a long breath, she struggled to find her voice. 'And what about Chris?'

He looked as though she'd slapped him. 'I deserve that.'

'That isn't what I meant. Oh, darling, you can't possibly think I was attacking you! For what? For loving your own sister, for caring so much? Don't you think I *admire* you for that? Don't you know it's one of the many, many reasons I love you?'

Curtis was at a loss. 'But surely——'

'But nothing,' she waved a dismissive arm. 'There's no need to explain all that. I understand it. Of course I do! I never agreed with you, but I did understand what motivated you. A combination, of love and guilt, predominantly guilt.'

He was looking straight at her, the depth of his love for her unmistakable in his eyes. 'God in heaven,' he said quietly. 'What a stupid, stupid fool I was in walking away from you! To think——'

'Curtis.' Charlotte held up a hand. She could bear it no longer. She had to know what Chris had said to him, had to know if the promise she'd extracted had been broken. If Curtis were here because he had his sister's *permission*, if he were here because Chris had persuaded him into it, then he might as well leave now.

She mentally gathered herself together, put as much casualness as she could into her voice. 'What did Chris have to say?'

'About what?' He looked confused.

'About us. About your wanting to marry me. Did she think it a good idea?'

'She doesn't know. Chris doesn't even know I'm in love with you. I haven't spoken to her for ages.'

Charlotte started laughing even as the tears brimmed and ran down her cheeks. 'Oh, Curtis! Come here, come and hold me, my darling. Hold me.'

He complied willingly, moving rapidly to sit beside her on the sofa, taking her in his arms and holding her as though he were determined never, never, to let her go again.

Charlie didn't try to stop her tears, or her laughter. Once, someone had asked her if she knew that it was physically impossible for a person to laugh and cry at the same time. She'd said no, she didn't. It had been news to her.

Oh, how wrong they had been!

Chris doesn't even know I'm in love with you, he'd said! Charlotte's arms tightened around her future husband as she cried happily into his shirt, soaking it.

Eventually, he held her at arm's length. 'What was all that about?'

It was important, very, that she answered him honestly. 'I'm just relieved, darling. You see, I—I hadn't been sure you were here for all the right reasons, here because you loved me *enough.* I mean——'

'I think I know what you mean. You thought I might have discussed this with my sister. And, if I had, you knew very well what she would have said. You were right about her, that night when you said she would have been appalled if she could hear what I was saying to you. You were absolutely right, Charlotte, and even then I knew it. Even as I rejected all the logic you were throwing at me, I knew you were right. You see, my love, everything you said to me, Chris herself had told me many years ago. I'm sorry. I can't tell you how sorry I am.'

He got up, moved over to the sideboard, leaned against it with both hands behind him. 'You must think my attachment, my attitude to Chris is bordering on the unhealthy.'

'I think it's positively unhealthy.'

He accepted that. 'All right. But put it in the past tense, because I've changed. It was unhealthy. It is no more. Darling, let me explain what's happened to me since the night—since I last saw you. But before I can do that, I have to tell you something else. It's about what I said earlier, that I need you. Charlotte, I've never needed anyone before. I know that sounds arrogant, unlikely, but it's true, and discovering that I need you came as a shock. It's a new experience for me. Consider my lifestyle; I'm "the boss" to dozens of people. I don't even have to work, I simply choose to. In one way or another, people have always needed me. And yes, there's Chris. She does need me to some extent, not as much as I've let myself believe, but to some extent. As you said, in as much as I'm her brother. But that's all. And that's all she's going to have from me in the future, the attention of the average brother to his sister.

'There's nothing helpless about her, there never has been. She's as tough as old boots in many respects. And yet I've always regarded her as my little sister, one who needed watching over because she's blind and because it suited me to believe it.' He shook his head, sighing. 'And that's been my attitude all along, even though she fought against it over the years. Well, that's all over now. I've let go of the past.' He smiled, watching her closely. 'As you'll realise, I have, finally, forgiven myself. I've finally accepted emotionally what my intellect has always known—that what happened to Chris was sheer fluke, an accident.'

Charlie returned his smile. She was proud of him!

'But there's more, Charlotte. I let you down and I put you through hell. You have to know that there was more than my consideration for Chris involved in my breaking off with you.'

She bit her lip. She had wondered about this, had felt all along that he had reasons other than the ones he'd given. Chris must have wondered about it, too. She, too, had been to some extent at a loss to understand her brother.

Curtis went on to tell her the story Chris had related, about his engagement to Julie Stevenson when he was nineteen, about the sudden death of his parents.

'It was a strange experience. Oh, I don't just mean the shock of my parents dying, I mean what happened with Julie. After Chris left the house and moved into Forest Hill, I went back to Cambridge. Bear in mind that when I'd last seen Julie, I was nuts about her, convinced I was in love. Suddenly, that was no more. When next I set eyes on her I couldn't even remember what I'd seen in her, what it was about her that had fascinated me so.' He threw Charlotte an apologetic look, shrugging. 'I'm sorry again, darling, but I was sure, certain, that something similar would happen with you.'

'Between Julie and you, seventeen or eighteen years had gone by. In all that time there's never been a woman who affected me to any remarkable extent.'

'Only because you wouldn't allow it,' she pointed out.

'Oh, yes?' His smile was a challenge. 'Then how come I fell for you, hook, line and sinker? How come I "allowed" it in your case? Why am I here, down on my bended knees and begging you to marry me?'

Charlie was grinning like the proverbial Cheshire Cat. Who could answer those questions? Who knew why people fell in love, loved, were right together, when with dozens of others they weren't? 'It just so happens that I'm extremely special and it was your good fortune to meet me.'

'Precisely!' Curtis's smile faded, his eyes searching hers for understanding. 'I was scared, Charlotte.

Scared, plain and simple. What I'd felt for Julie was nothing compared to my feelings for you. When I was in New York I could hardly think straight. I'd never been so preoccupied, so inefficient in my life. I missed you as I'd never missed anyone before. To the extent that I was furious with myself. I picked up the phone to call you a dozen times and I made myself put it down again. I fought against my feelings for you. They made me feel less than independent, something I'm not used to. I have to be honest, at that point I thought I would get over it once I'd bedded you. I thought much of my fascination involved the physical.'

'It does.'

He threw back his head, laughing at her. 'Of course it does, you wretch! But I love your mind more than I love your body. However,' he added, his eyes brilliant with amusement, 'that might change once I've—er—made further investigations.'

She was about to make a witty retort, but he went on, serious again. 'About that night, Charlotte. When I got back from New York. When I finally got to the gallery, when I saw you ... standing there, incredibly beautiful and ... well, it was then that I realised I was in love with you. As you were with me. I saw that, too, and I was overwhelmed. I told you that, didn't I? I was overwhelmed by all of it. You, me, the wonder of it.

'Then, later, when that idiot neighbour of yours interrupted us, I—oh, I don't know! I came down to earth with a crash. I asked myself what the hell I thought I was doing. To both of us. You see, darling, I also felt I didn't deserve such happiness. That was part of my guilt, of course. And at another level I didn't believe it could be real, that it would last. It had all happened so quickly, in a matter of a few weeks. Marrying you had not yet entered my thinking.'

'And I got heavy. I frightened you off. It was too

soon, too fast for you.' Charlotte looked down at the floor, understanding him very, very well. Curtis Maxwell was a complex man, a man who had lived for many years with an attitude of mind which was a habit.

It was as though he read her thoughts. 'I was fixed in my thinking—we both see that now, don't we? So fixed, so rigid that it's taken me all this time to come to my senses. I had to adjust, I suppose. No, that's not accurate. I didn't have to adjust, because as time passed I found I had no choice in the matter. Try as I might, and I did, all this time, I couldn't get you out of my mind. What I had to do was learn to accept.' He smiled, his gentle smile. 'In other words, Miss Charlotte Amanda Graham, B.A., I'm under your spell. I'm crazy about you. I need you and I love it! Now, come here . . .'

'No.'

'*What* did you say, madam?'

'I said, no!' Giggling, Charlotte was already on her way to the kitchen for more lager. 'Not likely! You think I'm going to let you kiss me when you haven't even bothered to explain why you were out with Pippa Loxley? This, when you were supposedly in love with me? I don't think I believe a word you've——'

She got no further. 'Why, you little witch!' Curtis's arms were round her waist, halting her in her tracks. She put up a fight, just a little one, before turning round to be kissed. It went on for minutes, so hungry were they, so starved for one another. It was Charlotte who called a halt. 'About—what was I saying?' Her voice had changed, it was husky with the desire he had evoked. 'Ah yes. About the other woman!'

Curtis raised an indignant eyebrow. 'And what about you? Sitting in the stalls with Geoffrey Hemmings?'

So he had seen her! 'Hey, that's different! It was only Geoffrey.'

'It was only Pippa,' he countered. 'Whom I find as interesting as a blank wall. Whom I find as desirable as——'

'Then why were you out with her?'

'Because she phoned me and asked me out, which I'm sure she later regretted. Because I was desperate for some distraction, because I'd had tickets to the ballet for some time. I'd booked them the day I first took you to lunch. When I got back to my office, I booked several lots of tickets in advance. In anticipation of your finishing with your play. I planned on monopolising your evenings. And you'd told me what you liked as far as theatre was concerned.'

'We-ll! You really were—are—the presumptuous type!'

'Totally.' He wasn't smiling. His fingers were raking through the glorious blond of his hair, made even lighter by the sun he'd been exposed to of late. 'That night at the ballet—seeing you like that, out of the blue! It—I didn't want to take the chance of it happening again. So I went into hiding. I had to get out of London. I took off for Amsterdam the next week, pretending even to myself that I was going on business.'

He smiled ruefully, reaching for her again. She evaded him. A new worry was niggling at her mind, just a tiny one. 'No! I mean—let's have something to eat, shall we?'

Bemused, he shrugged. 'If you insist. What's the matter?'

'Nothing,' she said lightly. 'I'm just hungry all of a sudden.' She looked at him, frowning. 'Have you got a change of clothing with you?'

'Of course. I've got a hire car out there, my bag's in the boot.'

She put her hands on his shoulders. 'Curtis, what are we going to do now?'

'I'm having trouble following your train of thought, darling. About what?'

'Us. All of it.'

'Ah. Well, that's simple enough! First, we change and go out in search of food. Then we come back and we ring your parents. We announce that we're going to get married as quickly as possible, tell them to start the ball rolling. I'm assuming you'd like to get married in church, from home?'

Charlotte nodded. It would be what her parents wanted, and yes, what she wanted, too. She was, however, wondering about the more immediate future—like today. 'And then we'll phone Chris,' she put in, thinking about the near misery his sister was in. 'Tell her the good news. And then?'

'We try the airlines. If we can't get a flight back tomorrow, I'll contact one or two friends and see if we can get a lift. Failing that, I'll charter a plane to get us home.'

'Charter a plane?' She gaped at him. 'But think of the expense!'

Curtis just laughed at that. Then, 'Perhaps you're right.' There was a gleam in his eyes. He slid his hands around her waist, hungry for her, unable to keep his hands off her. 'Maybe we should stay here for a few days, wait until we can get a commercial flight. At this time of year it will be tricky. But there's everything we need here, isn't there? Sun, sea, a swimming-pool . . .' He turned, glancing towards the bedrooms.

'Oh, no!' She wriggled away from him, embarrassed.

'Charlotte?' Curtis caught hold of her and when he turned her round to look at her, she was blushing furiously. 'What *is* it?' He was no longer laughing. 'Darling, please, something's wrong. What is it?'

Her cheeks were crimson. But she had to tell him, there was no way she could evade him. 'It's——' She cleared her throat. 'Just your timing. We can't start our honeymoon today. I—er—if you'd arrived a few days earlier, a few days later . . .'

Curtis was roaring with laughter. Then he was hugging her, covering her face with kisses. 'You sweet, darling idiot! Why on earth are you blushing like that?'

She didn't know, really. She just was.

'Come on, then.' He gave her a swift kiss on the nose. 'Go and get changed. If I can't make love to you, I can at least feed you!'

Charlotte took a shower, she stood under the jets of water with her heart singing for pure joy. Chris was in her thoughts again. She couldn't wait to speak to her, to tell her what had happened. Curtis's sister was going to be one very happy lady. Another happy lady!

They didn't eat at the apartments, they got in the car and drove along the coast until they found a pretty-looking restaurant where they could eat outside. Charlotte, whose appetite had always been enormous, ate until she was filled to the gills. She pushed her final plate aside, looked up to find Curtis watching her.

'I think your father was right.' He shook his head in amazement. 'You do eat like a horse. Ah, but you do it so daintily!'

'It's just that I'm going to cost you a fortune in food.'

'A fortune. What will it be like when you're pregnant, eating for two?'

'We'll have to wait and see.' *Chris*. She had to tell him about her conversation with Chris. 'Darling, I went to see Chris last Sunday. She phoned me, asked if she could talk to me.'

He didn't seem particularly surprised. 'She must have thought my behaviour odd these past couple of weeks.'

'On the contrary, she knows exactly, or rather she knew exactly, where you're at.'

That didn't surprise him, either. 'Does she know I'm in love with you?'

'She knew it before you did.' Charlotte was smiling, remembering. 'She's an amazing woman, Curtis.'

'Isn't she just?'

'But I'll get used to her!' She started laughing.

'What's the joke?' Curtis was laughing, too.

They reached for each other's hand under the table at precisely the same time. Charlotte told him about her conversation with Chris, to which he said very little. There was nothing he could add. Except . . .

'Curtis, will you tell me now, about Fernando Licer? I'm intrigued, desperately intrigued!'

He squeezed her hand, teasing her. 'Desperately, eh? We can't have that! What is it you want to know, my darling love?'

'Well, Chris told me about *The Lady in White*, about how Licer was staying at your home. I understand now why that particular painting means a lot to her, why she keeps it. But is it because it's your mother that you didn't want any publicity about it?'

'Partly. That was Chris's idea. She didn't want to be bothered with questions from anyone—about the painting, I mean. Nor did she want anyone to contact her making a bid for it. Licer's work is going to be worth a great deal of money in the coming years. Naturally, neither I nor Chris would part with that portrait.'

'And?' Charlotte probed. 'What else?'

He laughed at her tenacity. 'You don't miss much, do you?'

'Neither do you. Come on.'

'The rest is speculation.'

'Those were precisely Christine's words!'

'But of course. We've spent hours speculating together.'

'About——' She hesitated, went on only when she

saw no frown, no shadow cross his face. 'About Licer
and your mother. He was in love with her.'

'You can see it, then? You've studied the portrait.'

'At length. Not that I could miss it. I saw it straight
away. Every stroke of his brush was a caress.'

Curtis was impressed. 'You really have got a feeling
for your subject, haven't you? O.K., we can safely say
he was in love with my mother. As for her . . . this is
where the speculation comes in. Chris and I were only
ten at the time of all this. We don't *know* whether
anything happened between Mum and Licer while he
was staying with us. My father knew him, you see, had
met him in the course of his work, as far as I know. He
commissioned Licer to paint Mother's portrait. Licer
came to stay with us while he did it. Except he stayed
rather longer than had been intended . . .'

'The series, the six paintings you put in our
exhibition with the portrait, he did those first. It was
dim of me, but until I was talking to Chris I hadn't
realised they were paintings of *your* home. Or rather
the grounds.' She was thinking about the series now,
the autumnal scenes, orchards, fields, horses, a fast-
flowing stream, flowers . . . and in a couple of them, a
vast, handsome house. 'That's why they've been
locked away, kept separate from the rest of your
collection.'

'That's right.' He didn't bother to ask how she knew
this. 'Which was another example of my stupidity as far
as that particular period in the past was concerned.
Don't worry, darling, I'm not going to keep them in
mothballs any longer. That's why I let Edward have
them for the exhibition—though it needed a push
from Chris. But I saw it was high time the world got a
look at them, *The Lady in White* included. It was only
fair to art lovers, to the artist.

'Anyhow,' he went on, 'Licer adored the house, the
entire estate. He painted the series first, simply
because he wanted to. Or because he'd fallen in love

and wanted to stay around as long as he could! Poor devil, he died the following year, dropped dead from a heart attack. One thing's for sure, if my mother had an affair with him, it was with the utmost discretion. Chris and I never knew it, neither did Dad. There's no question about that.'

'Chris said your father was crazy about your mother.'

'Absolutely. And I believe she felt the same way about him.'

'You believe?'

'What am I to think?' He shrugged. 'How can I reconcile it all? Chris reckons that one can be in love with two people at the same time. I don't believe it.'

'I'd opt for something roughly in the middle,' Charlotte told him. 'I think one can love two people at the same time. It's rather different. And what would you know?' she teased, 'you're a novice on this subject.'

'Is that a fact?' He was laughing at her. 'And you're an expert, I suppose?'

'Give me time.'

'Oh, I will, my darling. I will! Years and years of it.' He leaned over, his lips brushing lightly over hers.

A youngster at the next table saw him and giggled. Charlotte glanced in her direction, caught her sudden blush. She turned back to see Curtis smiling at the girl, who was only nine or ten years old.

'Curtis Maxwell, you are the limit! I know you have a weakness for pretty girls, but really! I haven't got you as far as the altar yet and already you've got your eye on a younger woman!'

'Jealous, darling?'

'Insanely.'

He caught hold of her other hand, raised both to his lips and kissed each finger in turn. 'Don't **be**. I'll never give you a moment's reason to be jealous. Now listen, about the house——'

'Your house?'

'Our house, if you like. I know you've only seen a painting of it as yet—but how would you feel about living there? It is a gorgeous place, there are no two ways about it.'

Charlie hadn't had time to think about this. Now that she did ... 'How big is it, exactly? How many rooms are there?'

Curtis took a deep breath. 'It has eleven bedrooms, a billiard room, a playroom, six bathrooms, and on the ground floor there's——'

'Hold it!' She couldn't get past the 'eleven bedrooms'! Her immediate reaction was to say no, that in her opinion it was far too big. But what did he feel? He'd been paying for its upkeep all these years, after all ... And Charlie was thinking about Chris. She knew the house so well, and, presumably, she would be a regular visitor once they were married. That is, Charlie amended to herself, remembering what Chris was like, she would be welcome whenever she *wanted* to visit. More than welcome.

'Charlotte?'

'I—don't really know what to say.'

His eyes narrowed. 'That isn't true. You've just weighed several thoughts in your mind.'

'Oh, Curtis!' she said laughingly. 'How come you know me so well when you don't know your own sister half as well?'

'Ah, so that's what you were thinking about. Forget Chris. She has nothing whatever to do with this. This is *our* decision. Now tell me what your instincts are telling you.'

'That we should find somewhere new.'

'I agree.' He seemed oddly relieved.

And so was she.

The house, like all other associations with the past, was being put into perspective. It should be sold.

Without thinking, she leaned closer to him, putting

her hand on his thigh, causing him to look heavenward. 'Charlotte, will you please remember where you are?'

'You're a fine one to talk!' She let her hand stray just a little bit higher. 'I was just thinking about numbers of bedrooms——'

Curtis took hold of her hand and put it firmly on the table. 'I'm only thinking of beds. One in particular.'

'—and how many children we might end up with.'

'Well, we're more or less thinking along the same lines,' he mused. 'Sort of!'

It was only when the waiter strolled over with the bill that they shifted themselves. Until then they sat in the sun, content just to laugh, and to dream together, to indulge in their own speculations.

Some five hours later they were winging their way back to England. British Airways had had two first-class seats available on their plane to Manchester that evening, Ringway airport being the nearest inter-national one to Kendal. Charlotte's parents were driving down to meet the flight. In a state of utter bemusement, no doubt! Their daughter was getting married, and, the day after tomorrow there would be her twenty-fourth birthday to celebrate, too.

Chris hadn't been at all bemused. She had said, simply, 'And about time, too!' She'd said it both to Charlotte and to her brother, the telephone being handed back and forth between them. 'But you must forgive me,' she'd gone on. 'Congratulations and all that, of course, but I have to go. James is coming for me in twenty minutes and I'm not even dressed yet. You just caught me getting out of the shower.'

When they'd hung up, Curtis had said. 'James who? Who is he?'

And Charlie had merely shrugged. 'Why don't we just wait and see?'

'Darling?' He was nudging her now. 'Were you falling asleep on me? Bored already, eh?'

'Hardly! I was just resting my eyes.'

'That's your excuse.'

'And I'm sticking to it.'

The stewardess was heading towards them, carrying an ice bucket in which there was a bottle of champagne.

Charlotte linked her arm under his, nuzzling against his shoulder. 'And I'm sticking to you, my darling. For ever and ever.'

**For the millions who can't read
Give the Gift of Literacy**

One out of five adults in North America
cannot read or write well enough
to fill out a job application
or understand the directions on a bottle of medicine.

**You can change all this by joining the fight
against illiteracy.**

For more information write to:
Contact, Box 81826, Lincoln, Neb. 68501
In the United States, call toll free: 800-228-3225

**The only degree you need
is a degree of caring**

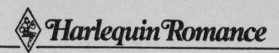
Harlequin Romance

Coming Next Month

2845 WHEN LOVE FLIES BY Jeanne Allen
The strong sensitive man sitting beside a frightened American admires her for facing her fear of flying. But Lindsey has a greater fear—that of loving a man who, like her late father, makes a living flying planes.

2846 TEMPERED BY FIRE Emma Goldrick
She's a young doctor, planning a quiet summer of convalescence. He's an ex-military man, now writing a book and planning a peaceful summer of work. They meet in New England—and all plans for peace and quiet go up in flames!

2847 FUSION Rowan Kirby
Despite her successful career, a solicitor, whose husband deserted her and their son, feels so emotionally insecure that she struggles against getting involved again, even when she finds a man she could love.

2848 IN LOVE WITH THE MAN Marjorie Lewty
Delighted to be part of a fact-finding team of Tokyo, a computer operator's pleasure is spoiled when her big boss unexpectedly accompanies them and thinks she's an industrial spy.

2849 STAIRWAY TO DESTINY Miriam MacGregor
Delcie, a typist, tired of catering to the need of her overprotective aunts, decides to work for a renowned New Zealand author at his sheep station. There she learns about her own needs . . . as a woman.

2850 BEYOND HER CONTROL Jessica Steele
Brooke rushes to France to rescue her young sister from a case of puppy love for a worldly, wealthy chateau owner—only to fall in love with him herself!

Available in July wherever paperback books are sold, or through Harlequin Reader Service.

In the U.S.
901 Fuhrmann Blvd.
P.O. Box 1397
Buffalo, N.Y. 14240-1397

In Canada
P.O. Box 603
Fort Erie, Ontario
L2A 5X3

Take 4 best-selling love stories FREE
Plus get a FREE surprise gift!

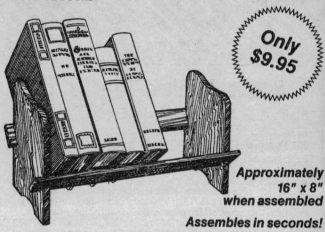